555

VOLUME 3:
QUESTIONS & CANCERS

CB555-08: 555 Vol. 3: Questions & Cancers
ISBN: 978-0-9962768-1-8

Carrion Blue 555
Chicopee MA / Lambertville NJ
carrionblue555@gmail.com

"This is Heaven alright, but there's a man outside with a gun."
—Cardiacs, "What Paradise is Like"

TABLE OF CONTENTS

THIRD FIVE'S THE CHARM
A Brief Introduction by the Series Editor

I was going to skip an introduction this time around since I barely knew what to say at first for this, our third installment, besides "It's a lot of fives, innit." But instead, I'm going to discuss the evolution of the series so far, and highlight some of the firsts of each volume, especially as they lead into some of the features of this volume that should be addressed.

The first volume, *None So Worthy*, necessarily exists as a first. It's the start, the foundation. Everything about it is first. But even then, precedents were being established that would influence the direction of the series: Nathaniel Lambert's *Phantom Trigger* started the story-as-told-in-fifty-five-chapters trend we saw expanded in volume two, and touched on here in volume three. For the purist, that might be cheating. "You promised me five hundred fifty-five different stories, you hack!" But I've always been sure to curate these contributions very specifically: each chapter, each vignette, should be able to be read as its own unique tale. I guarantee if you flip to any single "chapter" in *Phantom Trigger* (or DJ Tyrer's *Dreams of Futures Past* in volume two, etc.) you will find pleasure in how self-contained it is.

This Head, These Limbs, our second *555* anthology, had our first repeat contributor in Amelia Gulbranson. That volume also saw our first dabbles with extraneous formatting and design:

most notably the white-text-on-black-page designs for the stories of Betty Rocksteady and Tiffany Morris, but also the splattered-across-the-page text of Michael Allen Rose and Andy de Fonseca. Andy even gave us our first story told entirely in hashtags!

Now here, in volume three, we see two new firsts: Michelle Garza and Melissa Lason, the Sisters of Slaughter, provided our first collaborative contribution with their *Musin' For a Bruisin'*. I am also very excited to have our first asemic inclusions, these by Rosaire Appel. As the math falls, I can get ten authors to write fifty-five stories each, and I'll be at five hundred fifty total. Five short for our 555 goal! So each volume requires what we've dubbed a "bonus five" stories. I knew Rosaire's work would be a great experiment for our series, so I approached her to do our bonus five, asking for five asemic pieces that, instead of words, contained fifty-five *elements*. I left her to interpret that as she saw fit, and I couldn't be happier with the results. Whether you extract a narrative from them as wordless comics, or interpret them as more abstract and poetic (as I did in Brian Warfield's volume two *Rotten Bed Nuts*, for a textual example), these pieces embody and expand the 555 spirit.

To that end, I'll conclude my remarks and allow you to get reading. See you next time!

Joseph Bouthiette Jr.
Spring 2018

This volume is dedicated to the memories of Rocki Revert and Tyler Durden Bonito McHugh.

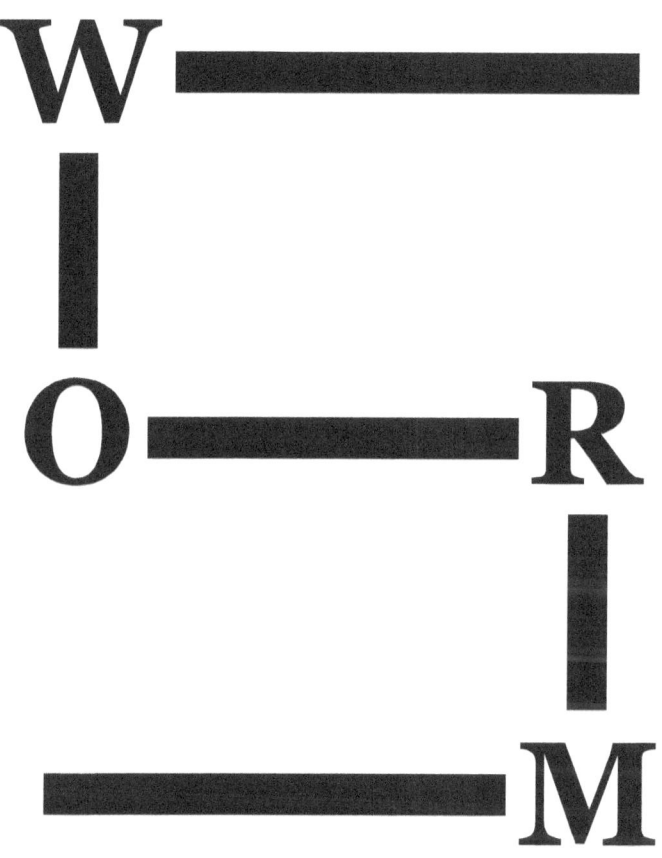

Dustin Reade

5

I was walking home and the sun was frozen in the sky. It had been like that for days. The news was all bad, talk of the apocalypse. People were looking for a sign. I looked on the ground and saw a worm shaped like a five. I knew this meant bad times were coming.

ALCHEMY

In the rubble of a bombed out McDonald's, we found a treasure trove of plastic spoons. The city glowed orange in those days, and we found incredible worth in the simplest things. Things like spoons. It was a sort of alchemy. We ate daylight and let the moon become a rusted jawbreaker in the sky.

EAR

We saw gunmetal horses running across the sky, dragging the corpse of the sun over the horizon. Gunshots rang out in the distance. You thought you heard a helicopter but it was only a hummingbird searching for nectar in your ear.

We cracked its skull on a rock and ate the jelly of its thoughts.

WHEELBARROWS

You ask me what I am thinking. I tell you I am thinking of a series of tiny planets, each the size of a wheelbarrow. I go on to tell you each planet is populated by children, one to a planet.

"How many planets are there?" you ask, and I tell you they are endless.

ASSHOLES

When you were a child, you say there was yellow wallpaper in your bedroom, covered with small, purple flowers. From far away, you tell me, they looked like assholes.

"It wasn't until you got up close that they became flowers again."

I ask if you would consider letting me lick your asshole and you laugh.

SKIN

When we at last realized the world was ending, we sat down in the dunes and let the sand cover our skin. You asked if we should give up and I said I thought that was what we had been doing. Lying dried out in the sand, we saw a worm shaped like a five.

SPINE

We walked along a narrow path until we discovered the corpse of a rotting giant in the woods. There was a river flowing through its finger bones. Its arms like a bridge and its back like an island, a rotten log formed its penis. We hopped over stones and spent the night on his spine.

CHEST

We were living in a trailer park. My sister and I would ride our bikes up and down the gravel incline. Once, I flew over the handle bars and lacerated my chest. When my STEP-FATHER lifted my shirt, the blood looked like dozens of Christmas trees. My family placed five presents at my tiny feet.

RIBS

The Easter Bunny lays eggs at the foot of the cross. The veins in his face straining. Tucked between his legs there is a tiny, imaginary penis.

"Forgive him," Christ says, watching the rabbit shit, "for he knows not what he does."

Water and blood spill from his ribs.

The Easter Bunny continues defecating, oblivious.

PETS

A tuba blurts a meaty sound into the empty streets. All the residents have abandoned the area, leaving pets behind. A man in a red hat and jacket swings a baton up and down rhythmically.

The strays exit alleys and garbage cans, thirsty for contact.

They construct instruments out of bone and join the band.

ANIMALS

A child writes a story. The MOTHER is concerned. A tale of animals twisted into unnatural shapes: horses with no necks, screaming at a frozen sky; pets left behind in the wake of some indeterminate apocalypse; worms shaped like fives.

The MOTHER tucks the letter beneath boxes in the attic, folding the horrors in half.

ANDY KAUFMAN

Remember when everyone died but us? At first it was fun but then it kinda sucked. After a while, we started pretending we were other people. I pretended I was Andy Kaufman and you pretended you were a dead body. I said, "Tank you very much," and you just lay there in the corner, decomposing.

RAIN

Once upon a time, it started raining and never stopped. It rained in living rooms, on school buses, even cemeteries. People's skin became waterlogged, pruned.

The worms jutted from the earth like limp vegetables. They bent into unnatural shapes. Most were shaped like *W*s, but once I saw one that was shaped like a five.

HEAD

I wake up one morning to find my teeth have fallen out. I try to pick them up but my fingers have fallen off, too. I sit up. My head rolls under the bed. The bed springs of my mattress are filthy.

The cleaning lady enters the room, sees the mattress, and says, "Dios mio!"

EARTH

The EARTH was fraught with apocalypses: earthquakes, floods, tornadoes, hurricanes, revolutions, explosions. People died by the millions. Corpses lined the roads. The survivors felt like giving up. They lay on the sidewalks and shriveled up like yellowed newspaper until their bodies drifted away in the wind like butterflies.

This, too, was another kind of apocalypse.

CRYSTAL PEPSI

It was 1993 and we were sitting in a swimming pool, drinking Crystal Pepsi. You said your skin was starting to burn so I checked the chlorine levels in the water. The whole pool was filled with Crystal Pepsi.

"We've got to get out of here!" I said, but by then it was too late.

TOENAILS

There was once a rope ladder connecting the EARTH to the MOON. People could climb up whenever they wanted and look at the EARTH below. One day, an old man looked over and saw a young man bludgeon his lover with a hammer. He cut the ropes with his toenails and kept watch there, forever.

BONES

The television glows a filthy blue into my living room tonight.

I can see the EARTH's bones exposed. I watch the MOON fall from the sky and crack like an egg against the mountains. In my sleep, I dream I am standing over the EARTH, with a hole in my side, spilling water over everything.

ARMPIT

To truly live in a world of arms and legs, one must understand the armpit, the crotch, the asshole, must be aware that the beauty of the antelope exists even within the pile of lion shit.

Christ dies all the time, remember: once on the cross, of course, and one million times on the toilet.

HORSES

The horses ran, frenzied, and leapt to their deaths over the cliffs. Their necks were bent at unnatural angles and their teeth were cracked and shattered. The cowboys cried into their hats, as the horses slowly decomposed in their makeshift grave.

A farm hand climbed down the ravine and planted blackberries in the horses' ribs.

ANTARCTICA

In Antarctica, scientists discovered a gaping hole in the EARTH. Hot, stinking gas vented from the hole, and it was soon discovered it was the EARTH's ass.

A small boy lived near the rim; every day he threw rocks into the abyss: one little boy, throwing rocks at all the shit the world can dish.

SNOW

It started snowing and never stopped. Trees stopped bearing fruit. Millions were homeless. It was a return to the caves. People huddled against the night in the folds of other bodies. Wolves stalked the frozen wastelands. All the livestock was carried off in the night. We became so hungry we started eating each other again.

STONES

The EARTH was filled with rocks. The core froze, craters in the dirt squeezing closed like pores. Worms popped from their holes and died. Their bodies bent, spelling our doom in icy letters on the pavement. Everyone saw only a single letter of the worm's message.

The World Will End 5 More Times, they said.

LOST

We listened to the radio until the signal was lost, and then we listened to the hum of the road and the noises of our bodies until that, too, stopped, and we were forced to listen to the oceanic flow of our blood pressure slowly building in our ears.

Eventually, even that signal was lost.

BLOOD

They were already in the water when their mouths started filling up with blood. The car was still parked near the shoreline, radio blaring. They had run out of road and, for some reason, had started swimming despite the fact there was no land in sight.

The clouds passed over the water as they sank.

THE CROW

There was a big surprise party and I showed up in a cheerleader outfit but everyone else was dressed as the CROW. Not knowing what else to do, I went in the bathroom and rubbed toilet bowl cleaner on my face and cried until my eyes were all black and I looked like everyone else.

PILLOWS

I put my face between two pillows and pretend they are my lover's butt cheeks. This is a kind of closeness we share: me and the pillows; me and my lover.

I start kissing the mattress and, suddenly, a puckered hole appears, just large enough for me to push through.

I climb inside and disappear.

GARY SHANDLING

We turned the TV off but we could still see it: Gary Shandling, smiling, his eyes and lips bulging.

"Make it go away!" you screamed, hiding your face in the blanket.

Gary Shandling started laughing at us.

I threw a towel over the screen but it was no use.

He was already in our heads.

RATS

I opened a bag of chips and it was just rats. Like, no chips, just a bag of rats.

I called the company and told them it was just rats.

"Well, have you *tried* one of them?" they asked.

"No," I said, but then I did.

It was pretty good.

It tasted just like chips.

CARS

When the last of the power went out, we were sitting in a bombed out parking garage, pretending we were cars. You were a Studebaker and I was a Jeep Grand Cherokee. The lights flickered and went out and you said we couldn't be cars anymore.

You said it was time to be horses again.

FISH

One day, the ocean crusted over like a scab, so we gathered all our fishing poles and burned them in the TOWN SQUARE.

The ghosts of fish mingled with the corpses of dried worms as we sang a new kind of song about blood and dust.

We danced while the fish swam through the air.

FROGS

I remember when the GIANT FROGS arrived: squatting on their back legs, poised to hop great distances, pulling not flies, but airplanes from the skies with their long tongues. I watched one pull a helicopter into its gaping mouth. The blades shredded its face, but still the FROG sat, waiting for something we couldn't see.

TEA

You were drinking herbal tea and your hair was falling out.

We'd run out of peanut butter weeks ago, and the cheese was long gone.

My bones felt brittle and my ribs were exposed.

"How's the tea?" I asked, shivering under a thin, maggoty sheet.

"Good," you said. "Warm."

"At least *some*thing is," I said.

SWAMP WITCH

The first time the world ended, I sought out the SWAMP WITCH and asked her to end my life.

I'd tried suicide: shotgun, pills, etc. But nothing worked.

She read my palm and said, "I'm sorry, I can't help you."

"Why not?" I asked.

"Death is not for you," she said. "You're already too involved."

RAISINS

All of my teeth were falling out but it didn't matter. There was no one left to see how ugly I had become. I had lost my fingers weeks before, and my eyes had shriveled into raisins the previous evening.

I asked you if I was ugly, but you hadn't said a word in weeks.

THE MONOLITH

The animals came and bashed their heads against the MONOLITH. It was just small animals at first, then elephants. Even the insects joined the fun. Their bodies looked like stalactites on the smooth surface of the MONOLITH.

No one knew where it came from, but no one could deny the pull.

Soon, the people came.

MANNEQUIN

Charlie sanded my arms down to the nub and then he walked over to the work bench and started fucking a mannequin. He seemed to really be into it. I walked over and watched for a minute, disgusted.

"Man," I said, "That's fucked up."

"Shut up, No Arms," he said.

Well, *that* was fucking rude.

GUMBALLS

Last week my GRANDMOTHER told me our family was one-sixteenth gumball.

"How much is that?" I asked.

"See this?" she asked, holding up my pinkie. "That part here is all the gumball you are."

I looked at my finger. I took a bite. Cotton candy-flavored ancestry filled my mouth and a part of me died.

SONGS

December came and all the livestock died. The children stopped their singing, their voices freezing in the air like speech bubbles in a comic book.

January came and all the grown-ups died. The children were forced to burn their songs to keep warm.

February came and all the children died. There were no more songs.

WRITER'S BLOCK

I had WRITER'S BLOCK and I was sitting at my desk when a tiny man fell out of my head.

We looked at each other for a moment.

"Who are you?" I asked.

"I'm an idea," he said.

"Well, you're not a very good one," I told him, before crushing him with my middle finger.

BABY

We pulled the baby from the ground but she was warped, deformed. At night, she screamed nightmares into our heads. Her tears burned trails down her cheeks and she refused the breast. We lay awake at night, asking what we had done to deserve this.

Finally, we dug another hole and we gave her back.

THE BUTLER

I am dancing with a woman made of dirty rags. A large hall with bones piled in the corner.

The BUTLER enters, carrying a phone on a silver platter.

The woman falls apart in my hands.

The bones catch fire in the corner.

There is no one on the phone.

The BUTLER bows and leaves.

WINGS

In the recesses of the HUMAN MIND, we find a STAINED-GLASS DRAGONFLY. The wings beat too quickly for the eye to follow, but we somehow manage to tie them against its sides. It fights against the bonds as we shatter the glimmering wings and destroy all rational thought.

The HUMAN MIND begins its inevitable collapse.

MOUNTAINS

We grew tired of the mountains so we tried to cross the ocean on the back of a dead whale. We ate the whale's bones and we slept in the crater of its head, crawling in through the blowhole.

One day, I asked what we would find on the other side, and you said, "Mountains."

45

When I turn 45, I am going to dig a hole in my belly button and crawl inside. I will build a house out of my ribs and keep a bit of bacteria for a pet.

I will live like this for ten years.

I will live long enough to completely devour myself from within.

YESTERDAY

So yesterday the Crow swooped down and grabbed a coil of my intestines and flew up into a nearby tree, holding my innards in its beak.

You walked outside and laughed when you saw my open belly.

I told you I didn't think it was very funny and you said, "Everything is funny to someone."

CARROTS

As it turns out, this is not my beautiful house. It is a hole. A simple hole. Nothing more. How I came to confuse a hole with a house, I couldn't say, but here we are. The two of us. Just sitting in a hole like a couple of carrots.

Two carrots in a hole.

GHOSTBUSTERS

Sunday. June. Late.

Everyone on my block is dancing to the *Ghostbusters* theme. It started earlier today and now everyone is dancing. At first, I thought it was coming from a car or something, but no... it is coming from the sky. It is in our heads, constantly repeating.

I have never been so scared.

555

555 years ago, a 55-ft. man leapt out of the 5th floor window of his apartment. The air between the sky and the ground was heavy, thick, so the man fell very slowly.

He fell for so long, his body evolved.

When he hit the ground, he had become a worm shaped like a five.

COOKIES

We danced in the abandoned Nabisco Cookie Factory in the INDUSTRIAL DISTRICT. The walls crumbled to dust, raining nails and chocolate chips as we danced through the fallen doors and into the heart of town.

We crushed a school underfoot, and a church. The police shot at us.

We danced.

We became cookies and danced.

GONE

I put the pizza in the oven and, to my surprise, it started screaming.

"Take it out!" my boss screamed, running towards the oven. "We gotta save him!"

He threw open the oven and started performing CPR on the pizza.

A coworker put her hand on his shoulder.

"It's no use," she said. "He's gone."

THERE

A FATHER and SON sat on a rock. The FATHER swept his hand over the valley below.

"One day," the FATHER said, "all of this will be yours."

The trees had turned to blackened stumps and the sea had receded, leaving the fish flopping in the mud.

"But, FATHER" said the SON, "there's nothing there."

MOUTH

After days of walking, we discovered a valley filled with the bones of dead horses. Blackberries grew from their ribs. You picked a few, but I stopped you before you put them in your mouth.

"Don't eat those," I said. "This is a bad place."

The vines shook like ghosts as we walked away, hungry.

LIGHTS

"You're a fucking liar," Charlie said, sawing my left leg off. "You never saw a worm shaped like a five!"

He cut a small hole in my abdomen, pulled a loop of intestines from my gut, and started hanging them around the room like bloody Christmas lights.

"Yes, I did," I said, closing my eyes.

TOGETHER

We woke up on a beach and did not recognize the shore. The water was filled with the half sunken hulls of massive ships. Steel girders—bent and warped—jutted from the unfamiliar sand.

You took my hand in yours.

"Where are we?" you asked.

But I didn't know, so all I said was, "Together."

Opposite: Rosaire Appel, "Undocumented Artifacts"

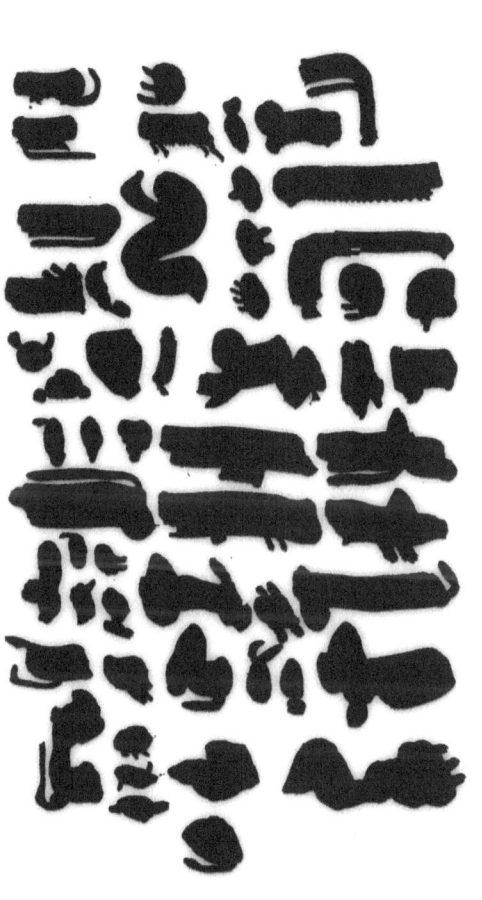

I
LL
UMI
NATI

J. David Osborne

EXTENSION

The cold exists mainly as a thing that creeps slowly. Air travel makes this different. At one moment you're in a place with a temperature, and then you're in a spot with something that transcends temperature, that instead becomes an attachment within the brain, an extension of yourself. My chucks are getting old and worn.

SPITE

Today thinks it can whoop me but it can't. I did fifty pushups. Difficult shit. I made myself a tea and sat back with it. Pleased with myself. I get scared when I talk about the day like this, as if it might do something to spite me. Spite is a feature, not a bug.

ESCALATE

People touch each other. Strangers do it, sometimes. It's seen as a friendly thing. Hey, we're cool, let me touch your arm, my friend. Escalate. Do not run. Put both hands on their shoulders. Run your hand through their hair. Caress their cheek. Find out where the line is, if there is one at all.

LIP

I watched *The Kidnapping of Michel Houellebecq*. I'm a big fan of the guy's writing. I love his ugly books. When I saw him on screen, looking frail, hair falling out, the way his lips look, how there's no top lip at all and this puffy slug of a bottom lip, I liked him less.

AGAIN

My grandfather decided to visit me in Portland. He booked his flight. I joked with him: "Make sure it's not too long." Three days before his visit, he got sick. Something with his lungs. He called me and told me he couldn't make it. Part of me was relieved. I never heard his voice again.

BARK

My neighbors have a husky mix and this weird little dog that barks at everyone he sees. The dog has met me countless times. He barks. It doesn't bother me. What bothers me is: the neighbors only let the dogs out into the backyard on retractable leashes. They don't actually walk them. I'd bark, too.

SOLDIER

Have you ever heard a soldier talk? They all have the same accent. It's almost southern, but it's distinct for how affected it is. The affectation of the accent is its most prominent feature. A large young soldier sat next to me and he sounded affected, he sounded like a child playing at being grown.

IS THAT IT?

I once paid $8 for a Corona. I asked the bartender if that was all I got, just the Corona. I think there was a joke there, something I'd heard that I felt like parroting. The bartender said, "Oh shit, sorry, man," and reached under the bar and came back with a slice of lime.

UNHEALTHY

If you do not know how to conduct yourself while sitting in traffic, or waiting for an airplane, or watching a pack of wild dogs rip a rabbit into pieces, then you have a lot to learn. Of course, I don't either. I'm not telling you to learn anything though. Learning is the most unhealthy.

PUT IT IN THE BIN

Feeling bad? Put it in the bin. Got a hemorrhoid? Put it in the bin. Where did your heart go? In the bin. Feeling tipsy? Put it in the bin. Sent a message that you wish you hadn't? Put it in the bin. The bin is over in the corner by the go fuck yourself.

STORY

The young man with nothing to say knocked up his girlfriend. They were still in high school. They loved the kid and sometimes they hated him. They both got jobs they didn't love, but overall they were pretty okay. They had a decent amount of money and lived happily until they died. Isn't that scary?

PIGSKIN

There's a man named Kevin who walks all over town. He plays football with himself in my backyard. Throws the old pigskin and then runs after it. Does the same with a soccer ball. Used to be an athlete. He got in trouble for hitting golf balls. He got mad when they cut his power.

VANNA

I was working as a checker at Safeway when this dude comes through just laughing his ass off. I ask him what's so funny. He pointed at the scratch tickets by the card reader. They were *Wheel of Fortune* themed. He put his finger on Vanna White's face and said, "Does she look like that?"

THE LAST OF ALL

I turn up the volume just a hair. The music feels good. Outside it is raining and I love nothing more than the sound of rain. I am listening to rain sounds on my headphones instead because I can control the volume. I turn it up until it's full volume... the last of all volumes.

ALONE

Sometimes I feel in my chest that I am sitting in a dark mall food court and someone has turned the lights up. Not bright, but I can see the grime between the tiles and smell the brown trash cans. In the background a grill is turned on, and an old man fries his meat.

LUSH

A man shops for his family. He buys them each a computer. He buys them each a bath bomb from Lush. He buys them each a life vest, but he doesn't want the ones that make him look poor. He takes the presents home and his family loves them. They all take bath bomb baths.

FROSTBITE

When I first visited Chicago it was negative twenty-one degrees. Wind chill. I walked out of the airport and called an Uber. It was cold like I'd never experienced before. I had some trouble breathing in the icy air. My fingers went numb in three minutes. A friend told me I could have gotten frostbite.

MEME

Social media is a car crash happening over and over in slow motion. You can't really say anything about it. The drivers will lean out the windows and hate you for stopping them. They want to crash. Say it over and over and you'll make it true. We won't die by bomb, but by meme.

FLIRT

I want to tell my wife, "Girl, you are looking thicker than Frida Kahlo's eyebrows," because I think that's hilarious. The problem is I don't think she will think it's funny. She will understand that I mean it as a compliment, but I think she will become defensive about Frida. So I say, "Lookin' good."

KOAN

A Buddhist monk once told me that I was a pussy and a coward. I'm still not sure about his credentials, but I do know that he told the truth. It got me thinking a lot, but mostly I thought, *what's the difference between a pussy and a coward?* Now there's a koan for you.

TRIP

Your brain is naturally flooded with DMT twice in your life. Once when you're born, and once when you die. When you smoke the synthetic stuff, everything around you slows down and then the fractal patterns start. There's no fear, no happiness, no sadness, just being. It made me not scared of whatever's out there.

CHAMP

I have been named dog-walk champion two years in a row. I don't know to whom I owe this incredible honor, but I'd like to thank the dogs. They are chill beings. I just vibe off their energy. Richy, Dulo, Agro Beast, Zone, Dora, Nathan Fillion, Trash Bag, Clancy, Mothra, Dominic: I love you bitches.

LOST

My friends and I got lost on a mountain. We walked down in the dim light of our primitive cell phones. Coyotes ran by, watching us from a careful distance. I fell on a cactus. A cop found us and took us home. My mother spent the night picking cactus needles out of my butt.

RAG

We thought the pills we were taking were filled with MDMC. But it was MDPV. A massive overdose. At first, it felt good. We spent days in a room. We put blankets over the windows. Cara forgot how to say words. She just held a rag in front of her face, trying to say, "Rag."

DOG PILE

If I take clean laundry out of the dryer and put it on the couch and walk away to do anything else, when I come back my dog will be laid out on the pile, taking in all the fresh scents and the bad ones still lingering. I now take time to fold my shit.

HEADPHONES

The first man the woman ever dated wore headphones during sex. She thought that was odd but she loved him. He left her after several years. She met a nice guy on Tinder and when they got back to her place, he popped on some headphones. All men, it turns out, wear headphones during sex.

GET OUT OF MY MUG

All you cats sitting in cups like you know your place. Get out of that mug and go do cat things. I don't care if you want to shit in a box or jump on a post or whatever, just get out of that mug. That is the mug from which I drink my drink.

SHOT

I knew a kid with Eminem hair who shot another kid in the back of the head over a drug deal. That sounds oddly cliché, I know. It's really strange though, to think about how he played soccer, and how he's never getting out of jail. Also, I guess, how that other kid is dead.

FOG

There's the fog you see on the beach in the morning when the air is cold and no one's out. There's the fog you see beyond the closest trees like they're sinking away. There's the fog that rings mountains. Then there's the fog in *Shadow of the Colossus*. Hands down the best fog, 10/10.

BUS

Riding the bus with the lights out. The blue glow of the dashboard from way in the front. Everyone is sleeping. You wonder how long you can stay on the dark bus. There's nothing to be afraid of there, nothing special waiting for you at home. But the bus is warm and it's going places.

CRY FOR Y2K

Everyone used to be crazy paranoid about Y2K. What if everything reset and computers exploded and we straight up went back to being fucking lame? What if we never got this beautiful thing bringing us closer? We cried out. We didn't know it then, but we were begging, in our own way, to be spared.

ROBOT

Life is simple: you're born, you go to school, you get a job, you fall in love with a robot that loves eating ass, you retire, you go on vacation to Europe, your robot that you fell in love with licks your ass so hard you cum all over your *Toy Story* sheets, you die.

CTHULHU

Out of the sea the creature rises. The sky is full of low-hanging clouds that signal its return to this plane. Green, webbed fingers and tentacles all in its mouth and shit. The reign of cucks is fucking done, you weak-ass SJWs. That's what I'm talking about, horror lovers: the beast Cthulhu! Watch your ass.

LAS VEGAS

Nothing quite like the smell of a casino. Weird feeling, lighting a cigarette wherever you feel like it. Women in small clothes bringing booze and so many lights and loud noises. Bros fighting each other. Streets teeming with old drunks having a good time. Poker with real serious poker players. I fucking love Las Vegas.

PURPLE DRINK

There's nothing as pretty as promethazine and codeine and Sprite in a Styrofoam cup. Some dude put nugs in the cup, which doesn't make sense to me. When I see the pictures on Instagram later, I understand: it looks badass. It all went down smooth as hell. The shadow people took me down memory lane.

TEENS

I realized I'd gotten old when I got mad at the teens who park their Civic in my apartment complex parking lot to smoke weed and cut up. I don't mind them doing that, but I became livid when I found the empty Pringles/Arizona tea cans they left behind. I'll bust those fucks yet.

ZOMBIE

We piled in and went to Last Call for the Halloween rave. I dressed up as a zombie. I felt that way. My jaw clenched. The lights were going like crazy. There's a picture from that night, and when I see it my bones feel empty and I have to sit there for a minute.

RELAX

He rides a lawnmower and runs a leaf-blower until six o'clock. He goes home and sinks down into the couch and feels the day around him and gone. The beer is good and he smells like grass. Flips through the channels but he knows where he's going: he watches *Family Feud* until he falls asleep.

ISOLATED

The first settler of Mars steps off the spacecraft and toes the red dirt. All around him the wind whips and howls across the plains and down into the canyons. Life isn't even a memory here. The spaceman takes off his helmet. Turns out you can totally breathe the air on Mars. "Tight," he says.

BADASS SWORD

The ronin walks the countryside. He is without a master. He moves from town to town, killing fools for pay. He sits on a little mat in a house with sliding paper doors and sips tea. He is ambushed in a snowy garden. He owns all of his attackers. He wipes blood from his sword.

MILLENIALS

I argued with a customer when I was a checker at Safeway. He said, "You millenials care about your feelings. You're so sensitive."

And I was like, "Dude, you're the one who's crying about having to use the chip reader." I left that job a few days later, but I still think about that asshole.

STRETCH

At this point, I'm honestly not sure whether I like sex or stretching better. Nothing beats waking up in the morning and reaching 'til your fingers graze the cold wall, and your feet point hard toward the end of the blanket. I'm going to start doing yoga, and yes, it is absolutely a sexual thing.

GRAFFITI

Pulled off on the side of the cliff and watched the fog roll in over the ocean. I took a picture of her standing by the edge, the wind moving her hair. We moved on to a little beach with a large fallen tree and under the bridge I took a picture of sick graffiti.

FRESH OUT

You learn when you stop it with the self-destruction that there's not a whole lot to talk about. That's the real challenge: once the monotony of life sets in and you have responsibility and you're not killing yourself anymore and there's no more coming home late hoping you don't smell a certain way, what's left?

PRODUCTIVITY

I look at George Simenon and I envy that kind of output. In my head I'm the guy who could pump this out without worrying about the words but really I agonize over each one, to the point that I hate the whole process. Maybe there's something past it. The only way out is through.

ELECTRICITY

I watched the Tesla coils trade blue lightning for thirty minutes. I thought it might get old but it never did. Outside the Hollywood hills rolled brown covered in scrub and I looked out at the smog and the city below it and wished I was born earlier if only to steal back the ideas.

CREAM

Nothing matters but money and its acquisition. Please get a job and wear your outfit and make the money you need to matter. Live your life full or destroy the whole thing. Follow the bit in the bohemian's mouth back along the reins to the man with the cigar holding the control, the final say.

GAME GUILT

One time a friend of mine got *Mortal Kombat II* for the Super Nintendo. I was forbidden to play this game, but I played the shit out of it. When I got home I cried and told my mother what I'd done. I felt so guilty. That's always been my problem. I should've stayed quiet.

SHARP TOOTH

"Just do the work" is meaningless if you're a dinosaur roaming the planet eating small mammals and looking for other dinosaurs to sleep with before the comet comes down and renders all of your feathers pointless. One day they'll find the fossils of your ancestors who had the foresight to die at the right time.

ROSES

Sometimes I'll take Rios to the Rose Gardens here in Portland. We'll get hot dogs from the food carts and walk down the stone steps and sniff each and every rose, running at times from the angry bees. We take lots of pictures for Instagram and the sun is always shining, which is rare here.

BACKWARDS

Most people confuse being an asshole with not giving a fuck. Folks on both sides tend to get it backwards. People give a fuck because they're afraid they'll be an asshole, and most assholes think that they're just not giving a fuck. It's a really delicate balance. Don't hurt people intentionally and you'll be fine.

NEON

There's something about brick alleyways and streets that sit too close and signs that jut out from the buildings reading neon splashed out across the night wet, they're always wet even if it isn't a wet city. I live in a place with lots of rain and I love the streets I don't yet know.

DAD STYLE

I found out that my headphones that I received with my Apple iPhone 6S have a built-in microphone. I've been calling people just so I can put the phone in my jacket pocket and talk to them on my headphones. Hands-free truly is the future and I'm sorry I mocked you nerds. Next stop, Bluetooth.

BALD AS FUCK

Britney Spears shaved her head and beat up a car. Natalie Portman shaved her head and fell in love with a Gamergater. Sigourney Weaver shaved her head and jumped into a pool of hot lava. Demi Moore shaved her head and got butch. Jodorowsky shaved those ladies' heads and gently pushed them together, because magic.

PYRAMID

The all-seeing eye on top of the pyramid lowers slowly. The point presses against the soft white of the eye, presses and presses, until it pierces with a pop like a busted grape, and the eye keeps moving down, it's all-seeing rays retracting back and fading, pink fluid running down the sides of the pyramid.

A YEAR OF
PHANTOMS

K.W. Taylor

WEDDING

Blood all over the walls.

She sighed and put down her cleaning supplies. Just another closing shift at the coffee-house.

Curiosity made her want to check the security footage, even though she knew damn well what happened. The same ritual, the same statement for police: "I wanted this. I chose death. Do not prosecute him."

SCULPTORS

"You make art?"

"I paint."

Her heart sank. "Never sculpt?" Would he get it? The code words, meaningless outside those in the know. Sculptors molded with lust, meat, and madness. If he were one of the perfect and insane, she would fling herself at him.

"Never sculpt." An edge in his voice, icy eyes narrowing.

EPIPHANY

The cocaine-heightened night dripped with inky shadows and too-yellow light bulbs. Desire thrummed, and her breath shredded itself past jagged teeth, rows of tombstones in her mouth.

The opportunity appeared in the form of a knife, glittering steel on the coffee table. She slid the weapon into her hand and took a steady step forward.

ELOPEMENT

"If I love you, I'll have to kill you."

"If you kill me, you have to love me."

The waterfall roars whispered promises to naught but air, each watching the other's lips move, grateful to be spared the revelation.

"If you love me, you'll kill me."

"Love me."

Hand cups cheek, thumb brushes over mouth.

NAKED

They slide into blackout from amphetamine mania. The mattress is stained beneath their tangled limbs.

She rises with the full moon, bones breaking and fingernails bursting into claws.

He stirs, watching her face split open from skull to chin, a hairy snout shoving through the cavity.

He flashes bloody fangs at her. "There you are."

PROSPECTUS

Her heart beats a last thump, blood spurting from gnawed-off artery, then sits, silent as wet, crimson meat.

She clutches the maw, torn flaps of flesh beneath shredded, sodden sweater, and drops to her knees. A broken rib cuts into her palm.

"Is it good enough?" she chokes out.

A boot stomps, and she flinches.

BEGGAR AND CHOOSER

"Wish," the universe said. She nodded and cast her face to the stars, shut her eyes, and put the desire in her heart.

I want a soul mate.

Two decades later, she is sitting on the floor of a two-room apartment talking to a ghost. "You got your wish," he says.

"Yes, but..."

He shrugs.

SOPHOMORE

"Lucky thing, catching you on your first kill." The detective sits back, hands behind his head. "Serial killers usually get in ten, twenty 'fore they get caught. If they do."

The man across the table shakes his head. "Yeah, lucky," he mutters. "Real goddamn lucky."

He thinks of the crawlspace and tries not to smile.

FALLEN

An old hell, a new hell, a borrowed hell, a blue hell... they converged as he woke with shackled arms, strange memories and rhymes flitting through his aching head.

"The plans, Agent?" came a voice in the dark.

"Go to hell," he rasped. The tips of his wings skittered beneath his skin, desperate for release.

PASSAGE

In a cavern, a boy wanders for hours, sliding fingers along stone, damp, and dirt. When he finds his way out of the darkness, the world is too dazzling, too bright, and he hisses, squeezing his eyes shut, shielding his face, missing dark.

"Come," says his father. "Adjust. The field calls your hands to work."

OUT

The elephant glared at them from its corner, snuggled onto blankets and pillows. It gave a harrumphing snort and blinked.

Mary took a deep breath. "We need to talk about it."

Derek nodded. "I know, I know."

The elephant's ears flapped back, rapt.

"I'm gay," Derek said.

From the corner came an indignant, trumpeting roar.

WORDS #1

His hair cascaded down his forehead, brow furrowed, as he pounded pain out on the keys.

The typewriter—squeezed between bony knees—stubbornly refused to make use of the whisper of ink left on its ribbon, and so he ripped the paper out and spilled graphite on it, smudges of sorrow, a flurry of failure.

WORDS #2

In the morning, he had nothing but nonsense, trivial leavings of a wine-soaked mind, and he shoved the lot of it into the fireplace before looking for a match.

But then, just as he was about to set his juvenile ranting aflame, he saw the words anew—crumpled, disjointed, devoid of context or cliché. *Alive.*

WORDS #3

Together, his words were trite, but rent up and jumbled, there was a keen, clean, mysterious poetry to it all.

He felt the first smile to spread across the hungry hollows of his face in weeks and pulled the paper back from the precipice, away from harm.

With scissors in hand, he set to work.

IN THE CABIN

The figure stood at the foot of the bed—shadowy, tall, masculine, and silent. Ken propped himself up on his elbow. "Bob, is that you? Go back to your room. It's the middle of the night."

The figure didn't move.

"Is something wrong?" Ken snapped on the bedside lamp, only to find he was alone.

AFTER THE CABIN

"Once at the old cabin," Ken told his brother, a pair of beers between them, "you sleepwalked into my room."

"Nope," Bob said. He eyed the waitress sashaying between tables. "Think she'd like me?"

"Your wife sure wouldn't," Ken said. "She ever say you sleepwalk?"

"Never." The waitress smiled at Bob, and he smiled back.

BACK TO THE CABIN

"This is where it happened?"

"Yeah."

Jill shivered. "Why'd you tell me?"

Ken sighed. "I don't know. Just in case it happens again. I didn't want you freaking out."

"If it was just your brother, why would it happen again?"

A voice whispered in Ken's ear: "Because you know it wasn't your brother, don't you?"

SUCCESS

The knight held the cup in his hands. "Huh, so this is it, is it?"

The old man nodded. "If you return that to your kingdom, you will marry a princess. You will be rich and secure, lauded all your days."

The knight raised the visor on his helmet. "Yeah, but, like, what then, y'know?"

PARALLEL

"Leslie Scott?"

"No, it's Lois."

The woman was in her twenties. Her black hair fell in a messy bob. "Yes, of course. They almost named you Lois."

"Look, I'm very busy, and I don't—"

"Mom, it's Diane."

"You have the wrong house," I told her. "I don't have a daughter."

"Maybe not in this reality."

THE IDEA

Her fingers drummed on the home row keys, and she stared at the clock. Words eluded her.

She picked up her phone. "I need an idea," she texted.

The reply was quick: "I'm about to kill you."

"Not what I meant."

"Be right over."

Surely her friend wouldn't... no, of course not.

The doorbell rang.

OCCAM'S RAZOR

"Sleep paralysis is a bitch," she said, struggling against the straps.

The alien nodded and held up a syringe in a thin, gray hand. "I warn you," it said, "this will hurt—"

"But it's not real."

The alien's black eyes narrowed. "Well..."

"*It is not real,*" she repeated more firmly. "I'm dreaming."

"Whatever you say."

THE WIRE #1:
WONDER

Bicycle speeds under football bleacher. Pale girl blurs, dark hair streaming out behind her in the wind. Then, a thrum and a gulp, and the ten-speed skitters out from under her as she hangs by the throat from a wire—invisible, razor-thin—stretched between two posts holding up the risers. She crumples, coughing, on gravel.

THE WIRE #2:
TAKE ME AWAY

Every now and then, the woman—now older, less pale, more blonde—awakens and feels the yank of metal against her neck, her feet reaching for pedals rudely ripped from beneath her. She gasps hard and registers her survival, precious and perhaps on borrowed time. She wonders what she's done to deserve this deadline extension.

THE WIRE #3:
IN THE TABLETS

"Gotta go." He's gentle, with big blue eyes and charmingly crooked teeth. He takes her hand in his, his bones bird-like beneath pale skin.

"So I'm dead?" she asks.

"It's not so bad," her guide replies. "No more traffic jams, and your phone's always fully charged." He presses a small velvet box into her palm.

THE WIRE #4:
SENDING ME

She opens the box to reveal a short red ribbon adorned with a glittering black crystal. He lifts it up and walks behind her. She holds her hair out of the way.

"A choker." He exhales a laugh. "Forgive my sense of humor."

"I was supposed to die back then after all? The bike accident?"

THE WIRE #5:
SO FAR AWAY

He bows his head. "It's my job to retrieve," he murmurs. "I saw you there, so small. I let you live."

"Were you in trouble?"

"No, but your fate wasn't as it was meant to be. And you affected others."

She cups his face. "You had to fix it."

With a kiss, he is forgiven.

TUESDAY AFTERNOON #1

I watch traffic. *Fall Butters on Sale!* a handwritten sign announces across the street, jaunty red asterisks around the words. Colored paper jack-o-lanterns pepper the edges of the window. A glass door beside the deli is adorned with a poster-size photocopy of Jimi Hendrix, expression eager yet sleepy, a striped scarf around his slender neck.

TUESDAY AFTERNOON #2

I watch traffic. My refrigerator hums to life, and six identical moving vans sail by in a row. I sip cold coffee and linger in procrastination, relishing the feel of failing to do what I ought. Stacks of books to read, papers to grade, and the contract to deal with. I pick up the phone.

TUESDAY AFTERNOON #3

I watch traffic as I listen to the phone ring. Soon, I hear the voice of the man who hired me. It's gruff, with an accent. "It's done," I tell him.

"Disposal?"

In the room a scant two feet from where I sit, the body dissolves in its fiery chemical bath. "Almost," I say. "Almost."

THE DINING ROOM #1

"I hate that this room is sealed up," the leasing agent says. She shakes her head sadly at the potential renter. "There's stained glass in there, and chandeliers. It's gorgeous."

"Have you seen inside?" the renter asks. She stands on tiptoe and looks to the transom window above the door.

"Only once," the agent replies.

THE DINING ROOM #2

The music blasts from the bar downstairs. Two in the morning. Chelsea's class meets in six hours.

Giving up on sleep, she orders cookies from the all-night place on the corner via an app on her phone and pulls on jeans. When she steps into the hall, silence meets her—so much silence, it's startling.

THE DINING ROOM #3

Chelsea shrugs off her surprise; the bar must've closed abruptly. It's quiet. That's what she wanted after all, right?

She pats her pocket to make sure she has her wallet and strides past the boarded-up dining room on the second floor of the building.

Only now, music starts up once more, and she hears laughter.

THE ACADEMY #1

"Rock and roll," she whimpered. The store wouldn't listen, though, resolutely spinning Muzak jazz—horrible smooth stuff full of too-perfect sax and over-rehearsed keys. She had to stay fixed to her chair, researching day job stuff no one would read to feed her true passion. Social science performed to support art was all too common.

THE ACADEMY #2

Every woman in the room cast plaintive eyes at each other. A sea of over-confident men ran roughshod over their meekly raised hands. An hour earlier, braggadocio assaulted them, with robust laughter and claims of having flagrantly ignored the reading for the day. Yet here they were, with much to contribute to the conversation—amazing.

FELINE

Hunger, palpable as a scent. She stretches one lithe paw and takes a padded step forward, a guttural noise ready at the back of her throat. Here in this darkened alley of vomit-stained bricks and flattened cigarette butts, she's willing to press him to the wall, bare her neck, and let his fangs sink deep.

MARCY PREPARES FOR HER PARTY

Marcy smoothed the skirt of her new dress. Mama loved this dress, taffeta and pleats, perfect for a little girl's birthday. She patted her face with Mama's powder puff. "Just cutting the shine, Mama," she grumped, anticipating the disapproval. "And you said I could wear lipstick." She regarded the sticks of pink and red, indecisive.

MARCY AND MAMA

With two slashes of red across her thin lips, Marcy grinned at her reflection, not seeing the days-old powder caked into the deep furrows in her skin, but instead a little girl over forty years younger, golden hair not yet gone gray. In the corner, her mother screamed behind the gag lodged in her mouth.

EARWORM

Trent knew he would never be able to hear whatever song he chose again without weeping. But he only had so much music loaded, and command said to put something on—anything—to drown out the screams of the tortured men. He scrolled through his iPod and finally, with a pang of regret, hit *Play*.

RED

She tugged at her scarf against pre-dawn chill. If she crossed this intersection, she'd have to wait, but if she crossed closer to work, traffic would be worse.

A man approached from the west, the sun not high enough to cast light on his hooded face. She shuddered hard and willed the light to change.

WOLF

A woman in a red coat looked around, and then she bounced in place at the crosswalk. He pulled his hood down further as both sun and wind attacked his skin, and shoved his hands deep into his pockets.

Hunching forward as cars whipped icy breezes his way, he sped up, already late for work.

THE TREATMENT

The countess stepped into the warmed red liquid as her maids stoked the hot coals beneath the tub. "Does it really work, my lady?" one dared murmur.

A second maid shushed her. "Beg pardon. Susannah's new and hasn't seen the results well."

The countess pulled Susannah close, leaving wide, bloody streaks on the girl's apron.

AGAINST EVE'S EPISTEMOLOGY

The closet was cold and dark. The clothes brushing her face were damp, too-quickly pulled from the dryer. She reached for the seam of a pair of jeans, the leg openings wrinkled up into clammy, closed balls of denim. Going by touch, she pulled the wadded material apart, letting the legs hang open at last.

DEBATE

If you can use that word, why can't I?

WHY DO YOU NEED TO?

Because without it, I—

WHAT LANGUAGE IS LOST TO YOU WITHOUT IT?

Without it, I—

FEEL EXCLUDED?

Yes.

FROM WHOM?

From you. From your art and music and language.

HAVE WE NOT BEEN EXCLUDED? WHERE IS OUR PLACE IN THE CANON?

POST-DEBATE

He left the dome, head bowed, and considered his options. Was she right? Was he wrong? Did he want her to be right? Why should he allow that, when history told him his gender was superior, and here she was castigating his race, too?

He radioed for a ship to take him back to Earth.

THE LINE #1:
OBLIQUE

"A line has two sides."

She wondered about his intentions. He wasn't noble, he wasn't credible, but he wasn't smug. There was humility about him she found appealing.

Her mother told her to look for the best in people and to then only choose among the best for herself. Was that what she should do?

THE LINE #2:
STRATEGIES

This man was arguably the worst, yet his acknowledgement of it—and his puzzling remarks —led her to discard her mother's advice as cliché and axiom.

"A line has two sides," he repeated. "Which side are we on, hmm? Or should I put it another way? Do the words need changing?"

"The words are fine."

MEGADRILE

The worm rose slowly and folded itself into a garish parody of a man, coils of flesh bunched into stumpy arms, and a flap of fluid filled, gelatinous skin wedged past its yawning mouth to form a grotesque tongue. "Come here," it burbled. "Come here forever."

Even as the creature sickened her, she drew closer.

QUESTION

She tapped her pencil on the pad, eraser bouncing against tidy blue lines. A question nagged at her, fluttering in her brain like a moth trapped in a jar.

She shut her eyes and let her hand move across the paper, heard the scratch of graphite. Then she switched the pencil to her left hand.

ANSWER

When she opened her eyes, her familiar loopy cursive spelled out her query. Then, just beneath it, small, tight printing slanted to the left. She had her answer, and she stared at it, the unfamiliar words she knew her hand had written, yet not consciously. But she'd made a promise, and she would follow through.

WE CONVENE IN PAIN

Six cats—hairless and pale, with squinting emerald eyes—flattened under the door to the carriage house. Their naked bellies slid against mud-caked brick, their tender backs hovered centimeters beneath ancient, splinter-ridden wood. The last of the half-dozen didn't clear the door; he mewled as a shard broke from the door, pressing into his flesh.

AUTONOMY

"Princess, awaken."

She opened her eyes. The robot pulled a blanket from her before handing her a cup of coffee.

She smiled. "You take such good care of me."

"You programmed me," the robot said, lights flashing in its head. "It's not that I'm taking care of you. It's that you're taking care of yourself."

CRISIS

Was something missing?

I thought of the radio, the short circuit preventing its use, and wondered if ten years in the future, radios would even exist anymore.

There was laundry to do, but then, there was other work, too, of vastly greater import. Still, the sun shone on the backyard—I could yet do both.

HEAT RATTLING IN THE DUCTWORK AND BLOOD RUSHING IN YOUR EARS

Tape your mouth.

Tape it shut, leaving you just your hands, fingers, eyes, nose. You can still breathe, you can still communicate, you can still make art, but your outlets are limited.

Now, bravely, cover your eyes. Slide a satin mask over them, reducing your senses.

When you can't see or speak, you must listen.

A TOAST

We closed her eyes and smiled. We pulled the sheet over her face with laughter. We giggled to see her in the coffin. We tittered as we shook hands with mourners at the wake. We kissed her cheek, chuckling at her. We threw dirt and flowers, squealing.

Her ghost lifted a shot glass and grinned.

THE NEW CLOCKMAKER

Karen thought of the marble clocks and the house with people trapped in its walls. A shadow moved across from her bed, and a chuckle rumbled through the hospital room.

As soon as she was discharged, Karen would move into the house with the yellow door and never leave.

The teddy bear's button eyes gleamed.

Opposite: Rosaire Appel, "Disordered Order"

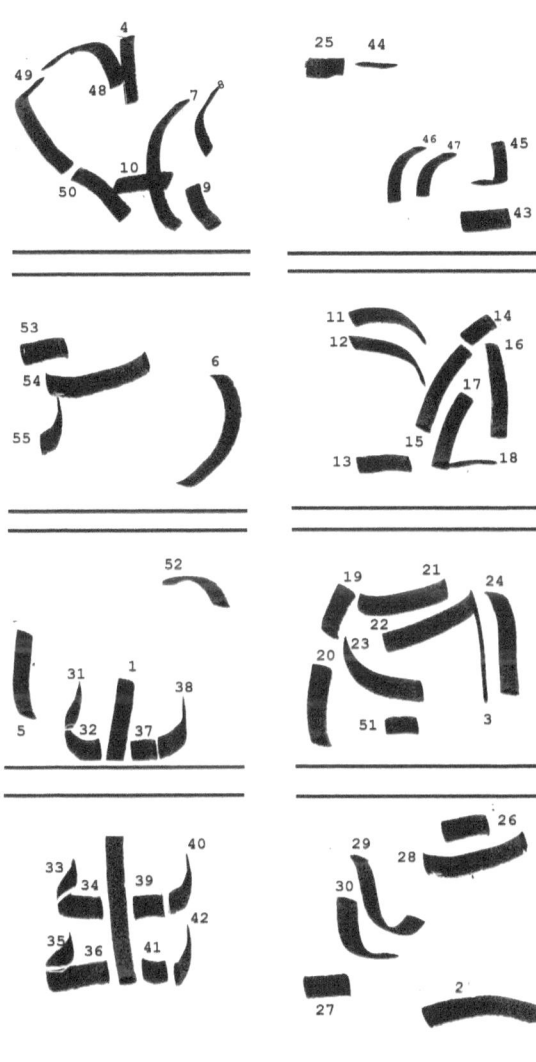

LITTLE GALAXIES OF

LIGHT

AND

PAIN

Jessica McHugh

DOCTOR FAUX

It's painful swallowing the pills.
He says, "Drink more water."
The tests seem excessive.
He says, "You can't be too careful."
I convulse on the table, spewing blood onto the floor, where he finds butterflies in the puddles. Singing praises for the grotesque, he wipes his fingerprints from the room and deletes his Craiglist account.

BEJEWELED

His ashes came in an oversized Tiffany's box, making him the most luxurious thing I owned. I wore him first in my hair like threaded age, then on my clothes like graveyard glitter. But public protests arose against my gray blush, so I moved him deep inside, precious and safe, far from life's dangerous digestion.

MOST LIKELY TO BE
BETTER THAN YOU

Kelly called me "dwarf" until I was a freshman and sprouted like a sequoia. She asked for weather forecasts until junior year before focusing on my stick-thin physique and I became a "washboard." I realized none of it mattered after graduation, though, as she cleaned this skinny weatherperson's ugly spills from the filthy bar floor.

CHILD KILLED AT ZOO

I met Daddy today. He yelled bad things about our zoo trip, about Mommy's budget and "welfare junkies." I didn't get it. I'm happy here. I saw funny monkeys and funny penguins. Mommy said I'll see funny giraffes, too, once I toss my Snickers wrapper in the trashcan by the business-man holding a funny knife.

LETTER TO AN UNWANTED LIMB

Dear [amputated],

What a drag you were. Each day, gleeful, you tugged me—panel, lump, and strand—into your sinewy cemetery. We knew we didn't belong together, that this would end with a dumpster and a crutch, but I was weak.

Still am.

I might stumble without you, but I'm stronger without your support.

Sincerely.

SILENCE

Olivia cried for months after she died. Her caterwauls shook our house, our car, anywhere she'd been.

The doctor had a tincture for the sorrowful din, and I guzzled it gladly, but the medicine didn't deafen her cries. It summoned her, and I watched, paralyzed, the grisly removal of vocal cords from Olivia's phantom flesh.

FROM INSIDE A TOASTER

I love Jackie Wilson. Despite the incessant tests, I can't stop dancing. I bop and worship the hope that this means more, that they care what makes me tick—and love.

They berate me. I'm slime, a disgusting slob, a weak electrochemical bond.

But I ignore it. I'll dance better, faster, alone.

...until Vigo comes.

THE BEST HEARTS ARE BROKEN I

I was arrested the day after he died. For hours I sat in a mirrored room with too many Me's while strangers watched from the other side with one swollen red cunt of a face. They grunted, vicious and baffled as a gorilla lost in the Rue Morgue, pondering how much a human can take.

THE MILO AFTER

Words and numbers aren't at odds any-more, and the kingdoms are peaceful. But I miss my friends. I miss my talking watchdog and the sky I destroyed on my adventures.

The doctors tell me to forget it, that I never left home. But it's all I have now: a padded room and plenty of time.

ORGANA

Mom and Dad are gone now. No codes will save them. No blood secrets can resurrect them or silence the roar of the masked devil who once loved my brother and me. As old heroes sink into the heartless dark, I will rise—a Princess, a General, shining brighter than any man or gold bikini.

THE NEW KAY

She lives in itchy glass that shreds my eyes. I know I loved her once, but now I only see hair on her upper lip, dimples in her thighs, her judgments veiled as compliments. I mourn how the old Kay saw Gerda, in the summers before the splintered mirror and the Snow Queen's ruinous kiss.

THE BEST HEARTS ARE BROKEN II

"Why'd you do it? What could you gain?"

"Peace," I said, but the mirror didn't know the word. It instead fluttered *murder* and *guilt* around the interrogation room like dropping daisy petals.

"He loved you not," it said. "Not because you did it. Because you waited until pain was a full partner in your crime."

TAME THE WILD BOOKS

Daddy took a wrong turn and made a bad trade—or so I thought when the Beast growled and tried to command me. He lost his power that night. He's just a man after all, subject to feminine wiles. Now he's a good pup, too, doting and docile while I'm curled up in my library.

ROBBERY GONE WRONG

The parrot is too still in the echo, head cocked, eyes frozen. Its beak is open as if poised to squawk but remains silent even as its owner stains the floor beneath. Our crimson puddles meet, and it twitches. There were no riches here—just him and me, our smoking guns, and a ravenous bird.

THE GIRL LIKE ME

She has green eyes, too, but the emerald's not as pure. They move statically and exhale plastic when she blinks. They show no warmth, never tear from pain or joy. They have no hard nights to scrape away. She is cold, just a copy.

So why does the programmer laugh each time he reminds me?

THE BEST HEARTS ARE BROKEN III

There was no trial, no jury of my peers, no table of cataloged evidence proving I planned or executed this grave plot.

The blame was undeniable, though, and I took my punishment in the form of life as usual—with one vacuous subtraction that trails every move like a moaning shadow of mirror and bone.

ABREAST WITH CELEBRITY

She was happy, I think, the last time her heart pounded my back. We were together, squished the way she wished when the cameras flashed and captured this unknown starlet for the first and last time. She was unrecognizable by morning, but thanks to my numbers, she is finally known by more than her surgeon.

EVERYWHERE YOU LOOK

It was the Bay, not a car. It was him, not a drunk driver. He took my daughters, my brother, my lover, shed a few tears. Now he flies kites and hugs away my memory.

Don't let him, Joey. Hold on for both of us. Keep laughing forever, and I'll know our love has survived.

BELOW THE SURFACE
SHE WAITS, ARMED

The forest sings her blessed name today in celebration and farewell. When the water closes and the silt devours, Excalibur will hear no more exultations.

Ages will pass, and the world will darken, but the Lady will not rise, nor her legendary sword taste the troubled air, until the boy king finds the sleeping lake.

GOODNIGHT KISS

There's a lady in my nightlight who knows my favorite song. Her electric lullaby quilts evening's shadows into a brand new gratitude for this iron maiden boudoir. Note by note, she infests and rebuilds me. She wears my insides like a beloved dirge, and we drown together in scorching melody beside the cold, dead bulb.

DUST TO DUST

I paid the crematorium to bake my best friend in an oven and prepare him for storage. Employees divorced, ailed, rushed to meet angry children, so they forced ash into a box that didn't close and a bag that didn't seal. Condolences for the slapdash memorial to my friend and the bad days of strangers.

A REAL CLOCKWORK BOY

The gears creak out the beginnings of conversation. His heart chimes, which pleases him, but when he touches the minutes rounding his face, excitement drains to fear. He cries, ripping at his spring innards.

Geppetto's timepieces have failed before, but as he winds down his new son, he realizes he'll never make peace with time.

THE BEST HEARTS ARE BROKEN IV

We didn't prepare enough. He left no instruction about interment, no notes assuming responsibly for his body's malice, but I gladly wear his shackles, which don't restrain so much as strip my flesh. Like plucked and soggy chicken skin, I'm torn deeper than marrow where I see him still, restless in my rusty, leaking wounds.

LEPRECONMAN

There's no gold at the rainbow's end. No rainbow's end, actually. There's only the arch and concave hollow of light. Inside the bow, color is too close to see, hazy and blended into shimmering mud that leads to nothing but the fools I've netted here. In piles they rot, claws still reaching for spray-painted rocks.

ZERO SUM GAME

She used ten fingers on fifteen thousand words over four days nurturing three characters eight books wide. She ignored her husband twelve times for two deadlines earning her four hundred dollars spread over six months. Eight fights later, thirty signatures divided their life. He got the house. She got meals-for-one and nine lovely lachrymose muses.

THE BEST HEARTS ARE BROKEN V

My prison is an old world with new walls. Every mirror is a bridge to hate, with unforgiving angles and creases and oily holes mocking my chapped soul. I'd throw myself into it, flay and shred myself to save myself, but the glass won't shatter. It only shakes, like laughter threatening a house of cards.

IMPOSTER SYNDROME

A vicious bitch with a puckered asshole mouth weakens everything that builds my smile. "They'll catch you soon," she says. "They'll discover you're nothing but a damn good liar."

I frown, try to explain my merit, and she groans.

"Typical bullshit."

I nod in surrender. "You're right."

The bitch's grin spreads, fortified and deadly pungent.

THE BLACK SPOT

They assured me you weren't really gone. "Stop crying," they said. "He's still with you, in your heart. He'll be with you forever."

My results came back today, and *now* they weep.

I cradle the x-ray, caress the black spot. "What's wrong?" I ask. "He's still with me, like you said. In my heart, forever."

THREE TONGUES A-TWISTIN'

Peter Piper regretted pondering the precise number of pickles in the peck he'd picked when he found Mrs. Piper and Betty Botter, their bitter butter-face neighbor, in bed with shore-side Sally, who'd sold her sandy-blond seashell to the wandering women. By the time he arrived, there was no room left for pecks, pickles, or Peters.

THE BEST HEARTS ARE BROKEN VI

I didn't cry today, so they dug him up. They made me cradle his skull as I sang his favorite songs. They photoshopped me into his old photography, like he loved me before he knew me, and I followed the lie outside like chasing moon-beams.

I'm locked out now, weeping in freshly shifted cemetery earth.

A BAKING ACCIDENT

Pie making is an art. You want the crust to crunch slightly before it melts onto the tongue and slides down the throat like butter. The filling should tantalize every sense and distract hungry children from worrying about who you are, why their parents aren't home yet, or the cracked molar hidden among the blueberries.

DOG EAT DOG

As Bobby and Lucy wail over their meat, I shovel in another forkful.

"I warned you if you didn't train the dog to stop barking by Thanksgiving, I'd get rid of him. Actually," I say, savoring the meat's natural spice, "I'm thankful you didn't. I hated his bark, but I am really loving his bite."

THE BEST HEARTS ARE BROKEN VII

The keepers told me to dig ten holes in which I would plant his bones. Teeth, they said, wouldn't sprout. Ribs might, if given special attention. But if I found a flower, if his dead parts turned green, I was not permitted to pluck or bask—for the guilty, they said, sow and never reap.

AFTERLIFE

"I'm afraid I won't see you again."

He kisses her cold cheek. "You will, my love, in the world beyond this one."

"But what if I can't find you? They say Earth is such a big place."

Fingers cross her sluggish heart, and he says, "Follow your map."

She's smiling when her long journey begins.

OLD FRIENDS

The cemetery is an old friend, muddy and rank and singing, "It's so nice to be loved, especially when you're dead." Fur and bone recall a Daisy who only knew dolls but now swings from tombstones into dreams where hearts beat and she's not here, alone in the earth, playing with stiff sacks of meat.

LUNAR GIRL

The moon terrifies tonight. Like split fruit staining the sky, it melts into her like a lover bagging for the first of many midnight dances. Clenched fists and locked teeth can't stop it. First come claws, then fangs and fur. Hunger comes last but unyielding, and her sisters howl for her to join the feast.

THE BEST HEARTS ARE BROKEN VIII

I'm sick. The house draws blood when I bump its mirrored edges, but it doesn't run torrential like a good cry. It's slow and flaking, like dried glue on an ancient kindergartener's skin. My keepers peel me free, searching my craquelure for reason but finding nothing.

My fever soars, and his lips are ghostly cold.

MAINLAND

The short hair horrifies her parents.

They ask for tales of her voyage but don't want the truth. They dismiss mutiny and murder, demanding she clean herself up.

She cinches her trousers and stands akimbo. With grimy tunic puffed, Charlotte Doyle says, "No."

They gasp, and she grins. Things are going to change around here.

THE TOENAIL TRIALS

Artists work with odd, broken things. Machinery and mirrors. Cloth, wood, and bone. I recognized my raw materials in Chloe before her first pedicure, long before my collection began. But those pale pink crescents live on without her now—a keratin castle that protects my muse.

See? Art is subjective, Your Honor. Like my innocence.

MAY I HAVE ANOTHER?

When the cuffs close and the lash falls, they're on their knees in worship. They'd prayed all day for this, all night, since the last time her neon violet nails clawed their backs and she said, "Get lower, baby, and call me Your Highness." They do, those royal submissives honoring their beautiful master's purple reign.

THE BEST HEARTS ARE BROKEN IX

My skeleton's a string for balloons of flesh rising from spots where his kiss once fell. Each day, my keepers verify the swelling sores haven't carried me away or convinced me levitation might lead to Heaven.

The wounds inflate as he enfolds me, but it's my voice that rises, booming:

"Who the Hell needs Heaven?"

ALPHABET STREET

They'd forgotten how to use those loops and lines and life-changing dots that adorned the last page of the last book they found on the barren avenue. They fed it to the machine, which sputtered and leaked an ancient world where words tilled the desert and sparked lively a dead organ above their hunched spines.

THE BEST HEARTS ARE BROKEN X

There are signs around town only I can see—new technology ensuring there's no rest for the wicked... or the grieving. I'm not permitted to say that word, though, unless I'm admitting regret for my actions.

I don't. Time has stolen it—a janitor tidying a burglar's mess, pocketing dropped gems like he deserves them.

SHAVASANA

Samm's Jams stinks of peaches and pennies. It ain't coins reekin' here, though. Or Miss Samm's feet protrudin' from the large tub of steaming preserves. A tabby circles my legs, burrows under the unfurled yoga mat, and paws the laptop beneath. Youtube is still queued up, paused but confirming the clumsy beginner's failed eagle pose.

JUST ONCE, WITH THE STABLE BOY

Margeaux fought her urges, aspired to chastity, and prayed she'd receive the unicorns' blessings. But nobody's perfect.

They sniff and snort air as she approaches, like detecting secret tumors. Offended, she lobs a rock at the creatures and orders them away. They do, but not before leaving blessings like oozing spiral tunnels in Margeaux's gut.

THE BEST HEARTS ARE BROKEN XI

If I try to wash his clothes, they'll lock me away. If I vacuum the couch, office, or anywhere he shed memory, they'll throw away the key. So I only clean the mirrors. They think it'll break me, but the cleaner the reflection, the more honest—a tearstained scab you mustered the courage to love.

A VERY SHORT STORY

Their disgust arouses him—bodies scrunched in offense, pussies drying at each PM, tweet, and dick pic—unable to stop his harassments.

But *she* can. Sorceresses are online, too.

The tweeted curse decreeing he'd lose an inch of cock for future sins makes him dry now, and he retreats offline with no harassments to spare.

AUTUMNAL ALTERATIONS

With changing colors and the promise of snow on a frisky breeze, October's arrival brings two important reminders. First, Thomas has to change the filter on his Brita pitcher. Hard water wreaks havoc on his delicate digestion. Second, he has to change the chains in Britta's dungeon. Cold metal wreaks havoc on her delicate skin.

THE BEST HEARTS ARE BROKEN XII

They broke the mirrors and my fever. They said I'd fallen too far into my own face, where false memories make us dig at imperfections. I see them now, purple and black beneath my flesh, but I love them now as you did.

"Don't fool yourself," they say. "Forgiven killers are still ugly as sin."

TRICKS FOR TREATS

While other kids dress up in the expensive, cheaply made costumes of characters they admire, Suzy will be frugal and inventive in dressing up as characters she loathes. Acquiring the raw materials will be toughest, but after some whacks, slashes, stiches, and snips, she'll walk the neighborhood in pride, dressed in her "other kids" costume.

HIDDEN KISS

"I want to stay young forever."

Mother grunted. "Yes, of course."

Flying around her, I said, "And I want a gang."

"Reasonable," Father said.

"And I'll kill grown-ups."

"What?!"

"They're evil, you know. Pirates. Like you two."

They couldn't protest. As Tink attacked, their shadows acted out the beautiful orphaning I would never, never forget.

THE BEST HEARTS ARE BROKEN XIII

Someone painted *murderer* on my driver side door, and I'm fairly certain it was me. At midnight, when the broken mirrors are dark, I leave notes to convince myself that I'm the only ghost here. My dear love doesn't know of these events. He doesn't condemn or despise me, because he doesn't know me anymore.

BLUE CHRISTMAS

One light on the Christmas strand died, and the others couldn't go on without it. In that darkness, our own little bulbs exploded and maliced December. We traded earth for plastic and adored its empty permanence. Our tree didn't live that year. Neither did we. And the family of dead lights mocked what we'd become.

GIRL OF THE CITY AND SEA

She can reach the kitchen from the bathtub, but the crowded space and boisterous city rattling her efficiency windows inspire no regret. It's good she left, and better she replaced her furniture with the gargantuan tub. When the streets howl and homesickness salts the waves, she sinks and unfolds her secret with shimmering iridescent fins.

THE BEST HEARTS ARE BROKEN XIV

They say I've served my time but I'm still a criminal. Wrinkles and shadows will betray me forever, as will my failure in allowing another human to unfold my soul.

But I can do it myself. Each day, remembering, forgiving, I can learn to accept this last reflective truth.

Some death sentences have no end.

FOME

UM DEUS FERIDO

Pedro Proença

TOURISM

This building has no exit.

I woke up alone in a room, naked, on a stretcher.

Now, I've looked everywhere, and there are no doors leading to the outside.

The windows are indestructible. I've tried them all.

If you find this, tell my family I love them.

And tell them to stay away from Earth.

TOURISM #2

Sounds, smells, shapes. The tunnel went deep, not just into the Earth, but into something else.

Several times I tripped on my own rotten bones, from earlier crosses.

The animals lurked in the dark, and I uttered a prayer.

Asking for safe passage.

I could see the finish line when the shadow blocked my way.

TROPES

People are rioting in the streets.

Windows smashed, cars overturned.

I marvel at what I've done.

"You will never win!" says the tied up superhero.

I shoot him in the head. Never liked when villains spilled their guts and then lost.

I'm a winner.

Murder, mayhem.

A new world is born, and I'm its mother.

MIDNIGHT INCURSIONS

The crowd chanted:

VENHA, VENHA, VENHA AGORA

TRAGA TUDO E VÁ EMBORA

I couldn't understand, but they were calling for someone.

Mesmerized, I got up and walked out.

The cloaked figures circled around me.

I felt my insides burning as one of them cut through my belly, and I became what they were calling for.

DIRTY CHINA

I don't like the look of this cup of coffee.

I jump in it, reaching a land of walking skeletons and two red suns.

"You shouldn't be here," one skeleton says. It has a long white beard and a red robe.

"Santa?"

"Yes, my son. Leave this cup if you want to live."

I don't.

THE CLOSEST TO GOD I'LL EVER BE

They showed me poetry written on a nut-shell.

I marveled at it, absorbing each word.

The oldest one laid his hand on my shoulder.

"Soon, this will all be yours."

I looked at the poetry, and worlds were born and died among the sentences.

"Am I a god of destruction?"

"Is there any other kind?"

OBSCURE PROG REFERENCE

When the Machine Messiah came, I was prepared.

"Here are my arms. My legs, my penis, my nipples. Make me a machine, make me perfect!"

I stood before it, a living torso.

The Machine Messiah turned to me—I despaired.

Its eyes were fire. My soul melted.

But my wish was granted. Mechanical life, forever.

PARENTAL DISCRETION ADVISED

I nibbled on the small rock that fell from the sky into my backyard.

Then I went inside and found my cardboard parents sitting at the dinner table.

"Jimmy, never eat rocks from space!" I said, mocking my cardboard mom's voice.

My cardboard dad said nothing.

I went to bed and dreamed of sea lions.

SAUDADES

I walked up to the babá, her white clothes and turban clashing against the night.

The spirit had taken her already. The voice out of her mouth was not hers.

I grabbed and kissed each of her hands.

She told me something I can't remember.

But her green eyes made me cry. They still do.

THE THING THAT
CAME OUT OF THE POOL

The thing that came out of the pool brought me a gift.

"What is this?" I said, holding the package.

The thing that came out of the pool shrugged and said something I couldn't understand.

I thanked it, and opened the package.

The thing that came out of the pool smiled and went back inside.

BALKHRULEY

When the Monarch died, his seven children laid claim to the throne.

The first: "I'm the firstborn!"
The second: "I'm the wisest!"
The third: "I'm the bravest!"
The fourth: "I'm the wealthiest!"
The fifth: "I'm the fairest!"
The sixth: "I'm the strongest!"
But the seventh just said one word:
"BALKHRULEY."
She was crowned the Monarch.

MYTHOS

Almost out of hope after crossing the desert for days, I stumbled upon the ruins of an old mall.

Mannequins were lined by the front door, as if they were greeting me.

I passed them by and looked for some food.
"Lost?"
The mannequins had changed positions.
"Yes," I said, weeping.
"Now you are found."

PERFECT JOB

The guards took me to King Kustard's towering presence.

"YOU STAND HERE ACCUSED OF TREASON AGAINST YOUR KING. WHAT SAY YOU?"

I spat on its face.

"VERY WELL, YOU ARE CONDEMNED TO WORK AT THE RECORD STORE FOR ETERNITY!"

The joke's on him, I actually love impressing 16 year-olds who will never sleep with me.

CONNOISSEURS

We all heard the noise, and we all saw the fireball falling from the sky.

A search party was organized to investigate.

They left for the mountains, and we waited.

After two weeks, I led the rescue party.

The bodies were lined neatly against the crater.

We soon found the artist. And it was beautiful.

OVER-ACHIEVER

I polished the trophy while the shape approached from behind.

"Aren't you scared?"

The voice was like gravel.

"No," I said, keeping calm. "Because I have *this!*"

In one fell swoop, I got up, turned, and showed it my trophy.

MCKINLEY'S SCIENCE FAIR PARTICIPATION AWARD

The shape backed away in terror as I laughed maniacally.

NAGGING

My punishment is to mow the lawn.

I spend hours doing it. The lawn is immense.

And when I'm done, the lawn is ready to mow again.

Repeat.

But now I've found something under a rock. A gold key.

I shove it in the mower, and it becomes my wife.

"Go now. You are redeemed."

BIBLICAL REVISIONISM

Lying in his tent, the wise man thinks about the falling star.

"What if this is just a natural phenomenon?"

Shaking, he exits the tent and confronts the other wise men.

They stab him and bury him in the cold desert sand.

And that's why no one has ever heard of Jerry the wise man.

FUCKING CATS

The cat licked my face while I died.

"Benny..."

Gathering strength, I lifted my neck and kissed his head.

Blood poured from my mouth, and Benny went away scared.

"Ready?" said Death.

As I closed my eyes, Benny jumped on the Grim Reaper.

"No, I'm allergic!"

I'm now a soul trapped in a rotting body.

MASTER OF PLOT TWISTS

"Breathe. You have arrived. Welcome to your new life."

I get out of the transport capsule and see out the glass dome around the station.

Lush greenery, mountains, waterfalls, giant birds flying freely.

I step out of the time station, and I'm greeted by my new tribe.

"Are you ready, Adolf?"

Yes. Yes, I am.

MEMORIES

My grandma had this little green metal fan.

On hot days, that little fan was a godsend.

When she died, I wanted that little fan, as did my uncle.

So I stole it, and rode it to space.

It was really powerful.

On hot days, when grandma was still alive, it was our best friend.

SAGE ADVICE

The forest was burning.

I gathered the kids, and Jack got Benny, our cat.

We rushed to the car, saying goodbye to our cabin.

"Step on it, darling!" Jack said. The kids in the backseat, still too sleepy to function.

As we drove, I looked through the rearview mirror.

"Karen, you need to move on."

BEST BUDDIES

The crows swooped down and took my dog away.

I chased them down the dirt road as long as I could, but they flew away.

Crying, I kept on walking until I couldn't.

The road opened up to an oasis, and my dog was there.

We drank from the pond, and I felt complete again.

CHANGE OF PLANS

They shot Johnny and drove away.
"Hold on, man, I'll call 911."
Johnny grabbed my arm and died.
I stood up and God nodded at me.
"Thank you," I said.
I flew, chasing the shooters.
They were at a strip club.
God knows how I love boobs.
He was there, too, getting a lap dance.

HOMAGE / PLAGIARISM

I stabbed the geezer and took the kid.

He was crying for his Papa the whole time.

I locked him in the cage, and went to get some dinner.

When I got back, he was gone. Only thing left was a bear cub.

"Man, I've read enough Stephen King to know where this is going."

THE JOYS OF FATHERHOOD

Joanne went into labor about twenty minutes ago. Now I'm pacing the waiting room.

The doctor comes out.

"Mr. Franklin, I'm afraid I have some bad news."

I listen, dumbfounded.

They bring me the baby, a giant cucumber with a face.

Joanne... I love you, honey.

The baby smiles at me.

God, that awful smell.

HERITAGE

The room was full of cats.

I picked one up, and it told me the story of my birth.

The next one I grabbed told me of my future.

Desperation sank in as I couldn't find the perfect one.

And when the last one was checked, I was ruined.

Father, why have you forsaken me?

ODD COUPLE

Leonard was bugging me.
"Are we there yet?"
"No, just let me dig. Stay quiet back there."
My hands were covered in blisters.
The shovel clanked.
"I think we're there!"
I couldn't wait to get rid of him.
The hard stuff was a chest.
"Is this it?"
I said yes while I raised the shovel.

OBNOXIOUS COMMERCIAL

There are geckos in the room with me.
I really hate them.
They conspire to commit atrocities while I sleep.
So I prepared a trap.
When they come for me, I catch them with my Gecko Glass (patent pending).
"What do you want from me?"
They snicker.
"We only want some flies. And your soul."

AD BLOCK

The video popped up.

HORNY GIRLS IN YOUR REGION it announced.

I just wanted to bust one out.

I closed the ad and browsed the front page of the porn site.

Someone rang the bell. Mumbling, I went to answer it.

HORNY GIRLS IN YOUR REGION

Despair took over, and I died with a boner.

EXTRA CAUTIOUS

We tripped the alarm. Jack and I ran, but split up at the entrance.

The store was at a small gallery. We considered the possibility of it not having an alarm system.

I managed to run down an adjacent hill, but I heard Jack's screams.

And a loud ripping sound.

They really love their jewelry.

PERFORMANCE ART

The lights went out on stage, and people panicked.

"Please, stay in your seats, help is on its way."

But people scurried and ran for the doors.

Bones were crushed in the stampede.

When the lights came on, bodies littered the floor.

"Okay, now where was I?"

And the actor resumed sawing children in half.

LITTLE GAUSS

The teacher asks the class to solve a big people problem.

Little Carl drops the solution on the teacher's desk after less than five minutes.

Reading it, the teacher says, "But that's impossible!"

"Suck it, pig," says Little Carl, flying towards the sunset, catching a ride with a comet to the end of the Universe.

LEIBNITZ

Like infinitely infinitesimal needles, he pierced my honor with his insults.

Therefore, with the promise of an especially rare strain of apples, I lured him to my alcove.

As I laid each brick, I witnessed his increasingly deteriorating state of mind.

"For the love of God, Gottfried!"

Dead, a virgin. So beautiful his mind was.

CRITICAL LINE

The critical strip is a harsh environment.

Surrounded by the void, I climb the critical line, half of the length of the strip, certain I can do this forever.

I aim for the heavens and, by God, I'll reach it.

When I find a ledge, floating to the right of me, all hope is lost.

ANALYTIC CONTINUATION

My machine was finally ready for testing.

A computer that could sum infinite series using the power of wormholes.

The world waited while I inputted the most famous series: the sum of all natural numbers.

Indeterminate series were easily handled by my computer.

But when I hit *Enter*, something appeared in the sky. Something unfathomable.

BARGAIN

Power absolute.

I read from the book. I chanted the words.

And God knows I provided adequate sacrifice.

But where is my power?

It's not in the whore's entrails.

Don't fuck me on this one, Demon. I did everything right!

...

Supernatural noises won't scare me.

...

You... can't be.

You're even more beautiful than I imagined!

THE CIRCLE OF LIFE

The warden summoned me to his office this morning.

I sat uncomfortably while he looked at me with his black eyes.

"Turner, you're free to go. Someone confessed."

I was speechless.

"Well?" he said.

I jumped across the table and bit on his neck. Blood gushed.

The guards seized me, but I was already transforming.

LOW SELF-ESTEEM

Chewing. I feel as if I'm eternally chewing on something.

I spit it out.

It's another me, crumpled up, clothes torn.

And she's also chewing something.

She spits it out, and the cycle repeats.

"Well?" I say. "This can't go on forever."

But the cycle continues.

I throw a grenade on the table and leave.

FREEDOM

In a darkened room, the conspirators gathered.

They spoke in codes, riddles, puzzles.

Communication was art for them.

The King watched from his throne, through the magic of blood and water.

Their funny way of talking amused him.

He sent in his soldiers to slaughter the funny people.

Their words meant nothing to the gods.

THE CIRCLE OF LIFE #2

Help, I'm being stalked by the homeless man behind my building.

I'm currently in a dumpster. I can hear him sniffing the air, catching the scent.

Of course, I only use the finest perfumes.

Please, if you find this recording: remember my earthly assets and physical beauty.

My name is Death, and I'm so scared.

OBSCURE CARTOON REFERENCE

The prodigy is up on stage, in front of the school.

"I've eradicated hunger and disease with some chewing gum, a paper clip, and baking soda."

Roaring applause.

"I've also created a thermonuclear device using my mom's microwave and some shaving cream."

"Wait, isn't that a *Pinky and the Brain* reference?" I say.

Then nothingness.

COMMENTARY ON THE STATE OF CURRENT CAPITALIST SOCIETY

I see the ninjas doing their thing through my monitors.

Don't worry, I won't engage them. I'm not paid nearly enough for that.

They acrobatically make their way into the main vault. I eat Cheetos.

Maybe I'll masturbate, thinking of that bitch Cindy.

She didn't have to be so mean when I asked her out.

BALKHRULEY #2

Calm down. Breathe.
You are with us now. You are safe.
How are you feeling? Can you feel your legs?
Can you feel your heart?
Just calm down.
Breathe.
We are safe, nothing can harm us here.
Don't mind the noise, it's just the wind.
Now, tell me, as a friend:
Where is the entrance?

HUMANS ARE REALLY DUMB

This party sucks. I mean, no one is listening to Death Grips, or talking about the latest memes.
What's the point of a party, then?
The house dog looks at me. I swear he's motioning me to follow.
I do, and he leads me to the backyard.
"Hey, boy!"
"Hey, yourself."
The beam envelops me.

THERE'S NOTHING WRONG
WITH BEING SENSITIVE

Sunset on the beach. I can't imagine a better sight.

Wait, I can:

A dimly lit room, full of grasshoppers.

I come in, baton in hand. I gesture and wave my hands.

They sing the most beautiful melody ever heard by human ears.

I start to cry. Someone touches my shoulder.

"Yeah, man, that sunset!"

REAL LIFE SUPERPOWERS

Banging my head to the beat.

The bass is somewhat out of tune, but fuck it. I have my girl, the place is packed, we're young.

But that sound...

I grab my girl and leave.

When the tentacles spurt from the ground, I understand the out of tune bass.

Having a perfect ear is great.

NOTE FOUND IN THE RUINS OF WHAT WAS ONCE KNOWN AS EARTH

Dear Karen:

I saw you sucking Bryan's dick in the shed last night.

Therefore, when you come home from work, you'll find two things:

My naked dead body in the basement.

And, hopefully, the hellspawn I'll summon to end you.

I trust you not to mess up my plans.

Sincerely yours,

Go Fuck Yourself, Cunt.

THE JOYS OF FATHERHOOD #2

My kid gave me a drawing of me and his mom for Christmas.

I wanted a Rolex.

We put the drawing on the fridge, regular parent stuff.

But the drawing started changing.

There was a Rolex on my drawing-wrist yesterday morning. And last night I found one in my nightstand!

I love that little freak.

CHILDREN ARE FUCKING STUPID

I was in charge of peeling the oranges.

My fingers smelled great afterward. I ran through the village, making people smell my finger.

But I stopped at the Witch's house.

A voice from within:

"Come here, child, let me smell those fingers of yours"

I ran to the woods, and wolves devoured me. Fingers first.

ALIEN ANATOMY IS WEIRD

I arrived at the Big Bang with some hours to spare.

The lounge was packed with tourists.

A mucous blob tried to pick me up, but I told it to scram.

When the show started, the blob was moping in a corner.

I gave it a pity blowjob and missed the beginning of all Creation.

I DID IT ON PURPOSE
TO ESCAPE A LOVELESS MARRIAGE

I just dropped my wife's favorite cup.

It's still falling, slowly making its way to the ground, where it'll be a million pieces.

My marriage is probably over.

I make the best of this weird time phenomenon, and leave for Paris.

My wife will never find me there.

So, from now on, call me Jacques.

LIFE'S LITTLE TREASURES

Children are running and playing.

I usually don't go to block parties, but I'm happy I'm here.

A beautiful brunette sits beside me.

She offers to read my palm, and I let her.

"You'll come by great riches by tonight."

One child falls, another one steps on his head.

I laugh. The woman nods approvingly.

LIFE'S LITTLE TREASURES #2

The salesman came around noon.

He opened his suitcase and I saw my house inside.

I stepped in, and the clock said 11:59 AM.

One minute later, the salesman knocked.

"You weren't supposed to be enjoying this."

I opened his suitcase, saw my house, stepped in.

"I love the sound of the clock striking noon."

ALWAYS BE POLITE IN THE FACE OF UTTER IRRATIONALITY

We're lost. We shouldn't have strayed so far from the trail.

"What will we do now, Jeff?"

Kneeling, I touch the ground, smell it. Put my ear on it.

"We go east."

That was a mistake. I don't remember a pyramid here.

"Welcome, strangers."

They're nothing conceivable by the human mind.

I smile and enter.

HERITAGE #2

I gathered my family for the last time around the table.

To my son, I gave my kingdom and its wonders of earth and sea.

To my daughter, I gave the realm of the spirits and the void.

They cried, emotions overwhelming them.

When they fell dead, I consumed their bodies, becoming one with NOTHING.

Next page: Rosaire Appel, "Illegal Parking"

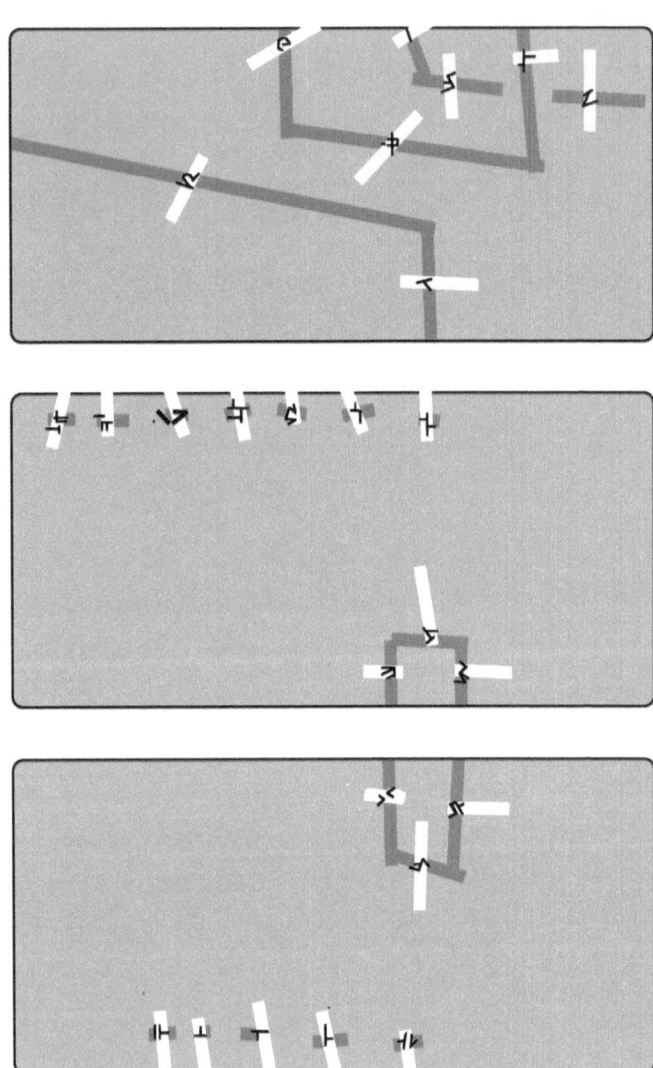

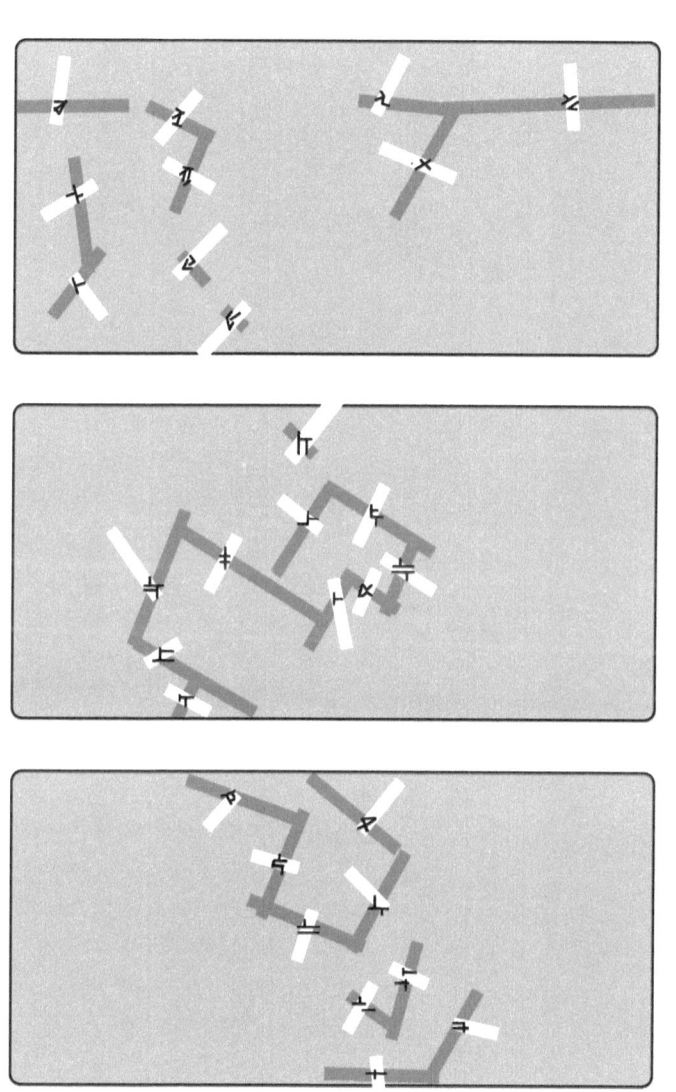

THE
PARASITIC
PRESIDENT

John Edward Lawson

NO MINDFUCKS LEFT TO GIVE

When televangelists rant about bad things happening because God has taken away his protection, I shrug.

Spiritually transmitted diseases mean nothing.

When I've got my spiritual dick in your brain I always wear a condom.

What comes next are fifty-four very spiritual moments.

I hope they're as good for you as they are for me.

CYNICA

She stands alone in the forest, the statue towering over her. It is feminine, of a robot, ancient and inspiring. Its beneficent expression implores her to take action.

She opens Facebook on her phone, trying to send the statue a friend request. It has no profile, so it must not exist.

She goes home. Frownyface.

PURE EVIL

Naked alabaster white relaxed and unspoiled in the dim light, the gap in its expanse filled by a widening pupil, adapting to this new life as a nocturnal predator of human blood, expanding painfully now, blood leaking from burst capillaries spilling down over high cheekbones, retinal damage permanently blinding, demonstrating the perils of biological overachievement.

DRAGON

NASA came up with a scheme to make up their budget shortfall: internet users could shoot down dragons after donating! "That's right, motherfuckers, not only do dragons exist but you can fuck their shit up at your leisure, from the convenience of your bitch-slapping easy chair!" That fundraiser was the most successful in NASA's history.

FALLOUT

The weather forecast today is a hail of charred bones followed by a dusting of blackened dander. Tomorrow will be windy with wings adhering to roofs as they dry in the merciless sun.

More donations to NASA are required to blow these bastard bits of postmortem precipitation from the air. Get on it, you idiots.

VORTEX

"All this is really unnecessary, it really is. I mean, look, I'm good at dragons. I'm the best at dragons. You don't believe me? Just ask any of the many fine Americans I have employed. Not only that, I'm wealthier than most of these donors combined. Sorry, that's just the way it is."

==>VORTEX ANNIHILATION<==

SPINELESS

"That's okay. A vortex can suck me into the sky or outer space or wherever this is. You know why? I have so much experience vortexing. Amazing experience, you wouldn't believe it. How much vortexing? More than my opponents. More than anybody. It's just a lucky thing for those dragons—"

==>VORTEX SPINE REMOVAL<==
...*FINISH HIM*...

HEX

"No spine? Rocketing through the cosmos in vortexes? No problem. The thing my detractors won't tell you is juju. I'm a friend of the jujus. I know plenty of jujus. I've got hexes out the wazoo on me, so good luck with that. Anyway, I've got so much backbone I don't even need a spine!"

PHANTOM DANCER

"I'm also the best at pole dancing. It's a little known fact that I struck out on my own in my youth and put myself through college the old-fashioned American way. Watch me pole dance on my own spine! And now I can do all kinds of jellyfish moves since I don't have a backbone."

CRYOSLEEP

A century from now the first human to wake from cryosleep will discover themselves in a world taken over by a former presidential candidate who returned from journeying through space without the benefit of either a spacesuit or a spine. Spine removal is a requirement of citizen-ship; this first cryohuman has already been modified.
==>SUICIDE<==

FSB

It worked when Zeus wanted to hook up with Danae, so he tried his old "I'll turn into a shower of gold to sneak in" trick... because nobody ever finds a shower of gold suspicious, natch.

In a Moscow hotel the future president crossed swords with a god.

Both Putin and Larry Flynt have evidence.

A NON-HUMAN HUSBAND

Goddess Athena was born from the president's forehead.

Tiny hands spanked her, even though she emerged fully formed, with lungs capable of fueling litanies against patriarchy.

A POTUS tweet went viral: *brEAstIclEs B 1 hEllUvA drUg!*

The goddess of strategy found he could parry every sword thrust with his old spine.

The honeymoon was over.

ANTS IN YOUR DEAPANTHS

...when lobster bisque doused her lap at L'astrance during the celebratory meal after her catwalk appearance and the burn pattern across her thighs resembled falsified WORDS OF GOD she knew her destiny was to be the third wife in the most powerful man's harem behind his mortal daughter and his godly daughter so she immigrated...

BATTLE OF THE MORRANON

He faces the assembled warriors, raising his voice to proclaim:

"One day face down Gollum up is how we will like to fuck... but it is not this day!

"The time will come when mankind will get jiggy without no spliffy... *but it is not this day!*"

And, swords raised, they charge into the rave.

DISTURBING SEXUAL DIMORPHISM

"Cave trolls, loose holes, Elven ladies 'bout to roll!"

The lyrics kept time with a brutally dominant kick drum.

POTUS gyrated with gelatinous uncertainty, tossing silver *tharni* at orcish pole dancers winging on his spine.

A battle cry pierced Goddess Athena's gloom.

She nocked an arrow, realizing news of the resistance's failure had been fake.

IS WE SICK, MASSA?

Hello. My name is Morgan Freeman.

I have no relation to that other fellow.

But.

You are, undoubtedly, hearing these words in his voice.

I'm okay with that.

What I'm not okay with is this Gollum-fucking and troll ass. So I'm chronicling this apocalypse so all the folks three million years in the future understand.

SPIDER FRENCHING

A female soul is not a male soul emasculated by grabby grabbing that pussy cookie dough pattern from the faceless mouth of an arachnid god that lives only in the hidden recesses of the Goddess Athena alone.

Bards sing well and wisely of this.

The three million-year battle hymn resonates through time with soul-killing force.

GET YOUR SLOB ON MY SHELOB

But still through the strife he was there, who existed well before Ras/Putin and endured well after perestroika: Morranon.

And Shelob the feature dancer surmounted his spire, from which heights she cast down her honor and smote its ruin upon his craggy features.

Doomed is he who getteth head from a non-human wife.

Chelicerae fellatio.

REBUTTAL FROM THE
AFROPOCALYPSE

Hello, this is Morgan.

Yes, that one.

And I'm here to tell you, as an octogenarian thespian of the African Diaspora:

Fuck y'all.

That despicable title of the previous story ignores the fact being faceless is the only way to survive when justice is based on what you look like.

So no.

We ain't sick.

ISOLATION

We're stuck in this ground level apartment during early morning hours with no power, and howls in the distance. Nudging the curtains aside to scan the wide lawn areas, but the trees beyond are obscured by darkness and fog. The werewolves have yet to force their way in, although they still manage to menace me.

DISCONNECT

Those goddamn werewolves interrupt our board game by lurking outside, making threatening noises.

"Don't worry about it. Just ignore them. You didn't even roll the dice yet!"

Sitting here in the absence of light with a handful of fellow squatters failing to adequately populate this apartment building: fun.

Calls to the police for help: unanswered.

PATHOLOGIC

As a social experiment a nude woman walks the city streets.

She is observed by a team of specialists who meticulously record visual, audio, biological, and atmospheric data.

She goes unharmed, but the specialists frenziedly assault each other, with no survivors.

Data in the observation room was unrecorded so the experiment must be conducted again.

AND ONE TO GROW ON

A giant eye appears outside Daniel's window.

He sees it, and, thinking his parents hired a dinosaur for his 10th birthday party, opens the window for a better look.

Massive jaws clamp down on him.

He is carried to a remote location, agonized screams unanswered in the darkness.

He is held down and devoured alive.

HONOR SYSTEM

I needed a friend, and using Deforestation Prime my friend was delivered with free two day shipping.

I could see why they had such good customer reviews.

I stabbed them in the left eye, stuffed them back in the box, and returned them for a full refund.

(I'm counter-culture, so I can't like popular things.)

FUCK THE WORLD

I grabbed my genitals, grabbed a gun, grabbed a religious text, grabbed a family-sized can of whoop-ass, grabbed validation via social media posts, grabbed some opinions passing as journalism, grabbed the steering wheel, and grabbed the last available mass murder slot today. I had to let go of my loved ones to hold all that.

SOULMATE

I had to kill my doctor.

She wanted to cut me open.

The worm growing strong inside me was her target.

My worm weakens me, causes pain, restricts my movement, and more.

It's been with me for decades, the only witness to what I've been through.

My parasite is the only one who understands me.

DICK EATER

He watches for weeks, noting her every move.

The stun gun is in hand.

The suxamethonium chorlide is ready for injection next.

The Hildbrant rotary tattoo gun is prepped to ink *DICK EATER* into her face.

She's asleep, alone.

He returns home content to know he's spared another person from what he suffered in prison.

WORST FUNERAL SERVICES, LLC

Every time they throw the lever on the incinerator at the crematory the body inside does not burn.

Instead... the world catches on fire.

Worst Funeral stays open, though, because some folks distrust investigative reports and, anyway, it's locally owned and operated.

Partially melted fencing holds back protesters.

The blackened world is full of business.

DISRUPTION

Werewolves congregate under moonlight, their talons scraping pocked bone.

As their Dungeon Master unveils their final opponent, humans inside the condo building have a bitchfit.

"What the Christ are they so worked up about," D. Harlan snarls. "I can't roll the bones straight with that racket!"

Hanna pads into the condominium to shut them up.

WEREWOLF WOMEN
OF THE DARKNESS

"Excuse me," Hanna growls, pressing the doorbell. "You dickless dickheads home?"

While no direct reply is forthcoming she can hear humans inside whispering to each other.

"One side, freaky boo, Imma handle this," Stephanie declares, throwing the door open only for onrushing humans to slam it in her face.

"THUNDERTITTIES!" Jessica roars at the moon.

CARTOGRAPHY EXPERTS

To his fellow werewolves D. Harlan says, acknowledging a map crudely drawn in drying blood, "Our target is below us—"

"That's not a proper doorway," Blake interrupts.

Hanna leans in. "Is that meant to be a dais?"

"Oh, for fuck's sake!" D. Harlan, exasperated, procures more blood to conform his battle map to D&D guidelines.

TACTICAL ADVANTAGE

Werewolves breach the ceiling, windows, and doors.

This kill team is bent on defending the sanctity of roleplaying.

What awaits them is roleplaying taken to nightmarish levels.

The humans lurk in teddy bear suits, and worse.

"*Furries,*" Blake cries. "*Pull out!*"

"That's not something I ever do," chuckles the one in gold tights.

Screams follow.

IT IS WHAT IT IS

The most somber game of Cards Against Humanity ever is underway.

Too many werewolves and furries are crammed into the darkened condominium.

Somebody played the "big black dick."

"You know it was supposed to be a card, right? Not literal?"

There is no reply.

A shotgun is pumped in a dark corner.

"Laugh, damn you!"

CHILDHOOD MEMORIES

The tray rests atop a freshly-ironed crimson table cloth.

The smooth, firm chocolate dome it holds inspires us to salivate.

Fingers coil around handle; blade penetrates dessert.

Separation, moist if forced, resonates... followed by gasps, whimpers.

The animal fetus within squirms, struggling to survive without its confectionary incubator.

Father's baritone blessing: "God damn, let's eat."

SILLY FISH

Orin spends time crouching at the water's edge, enjoying the marsh's stillness.

Occasionally things stare back, wide-eyed and wistful.

He smiles. They joke about him digging up dead things for them to consume.

Wait until he tells his schoolmates after summer break! These silly fish think he's grown up to be doing things like that.

HAPPILY EVER AFTER, AND AFTER, AND AFTER

The world never ends when you want it to.

With each fresh violation of your flesh, autonomy, and morals your body does not expire, nor does your memory falter.

Your shame is amplified by sunlight, drowning out all other voices as it scalds you.

The braille of your scars tells a story destined for obscurity.

BRAZILIAN DEFORESTATION

This piece of skin is yours now.

It came from my right testes.

Recognize the tell-tale shape from peeling via cheese grater?

Hold still for the stapler. Your tongue is hard enough to grab.

Look at this: my tongue, grater... your vulva.

Getting that skin won't be easy, but one day we'll laugh about this.

CHEERFUL PAIN

The only honest holiday of the season is upon us.

Employing a Cheerful Pain Knife I carve my own layers of skin, fat, and muscle.

Each day for a month we all expose a new organ, holding things in place with pins, staples, or festive glittering glue.

It culminates with the gift of fewer acquaintances.

CRIMINALIZED FRENCH

Hello, it says in your materials that hair regrowth should be noticeable within a month.

That's correct. Where exactly are you—

My tongue.

It's for external use only!

I mean, it's going on a girl's vag stapled to my tongue.

That's why you sound funny. I'm transferring you to your local sheriff for assistance.

Thanks.

SILLY STORIES

Kuame grows weary of Orin regaling him about the "silly fish" and ventures into the wetlands surrounding their community.

He finds the spot, kneels on stone, observes. Sure enough: orange masses, round and fleshy, drift toward him with fish scales, yet no fins. Countless tendrils propel them.

He flees, haunted by their disproportionately large eyes.

IDEALISM PAYS OFF

Silly fish dance around Orin as he stands in water, happy.

One hovers nearby, staring with protuberant eyes.

"Hey there, boy," it says.

"Yeah, *baby*, do I get like a reward or what?"

"Yes. Let me kiss your hand."

Orin dips his hand toward it, permitting just that.

Instantly he feels unwell, and staggers away.

MYCOBACTERIUM LEPRAE X

"Well, doctor?"

"I think we're looking at something more severe than psoriasis. I just got off the phone with the Emerging Infections Program here in Maryland, and—"

"You what? My son doesn't have some disease!"

"Ma'am, I think you'd best have a seat. And Orin... could you go stand over there please? No, farther. Thanks."

THE LITTLE STORIES
OF HOW PEOPLE RESIST

It was Terkel's job to sharpen pencils.

Every day he would go through his supply and ensure one in five pencils did not get sharpened.

The secret thrill he felt at day's end when the pencils were shipped out never dulled.

The regime fell within 12 years.

Coincidence?

No act of defiance is too small.

IT'S EXTREME TO SAY
THAT COULD HAPPEN

The first time somebody wanted to strip search me I was four years old.

They ran the 7-11 in our neighborhood. We were of different races.

My mother was shopping while I looked at comic books.

It wasn't too long before that place closed and a new 7-11 opened down the road under different ownership.

LV

Agrippina, your son is a damn monster and you know it.

You try to outmaneuver each other, poisoning as you go.

Your family leaves a trail of bodies in its wake.

Your control over him slips, and Nero becomes his own man.

"Smite my womb" will be your last words, although the assassin didn't comply.

DLV

Erb of Gwent died.

Can I just say?

How do you go around being named Erb of Gwent and *not* expect to die?

Fucking seriously. Maybe I'm xenophobic, or just a hater, but Theudabald also died.

These guys were kings. I'm lucky if I can just get a sandwich, even though they aren't officially invented.

MCMLV

We are sending U.S. Military Assistance Advisory Group experts in order to avoid war spreading and destabilizing the region.

Vietnam will not fall out of the benevolent rule of our friends, the French, if we act judiciously now.

The security of democracy in the world depends on swift, successful action—history will bear this out.

2011

You are somewhere out there not reading this, but I needed to tell you that you saved my life.

You gave me a future and hope and reignited my love for myself.

I hope one day you find all of that, and more, for yourself—if you haven't already.

You are loved, now and forever.

TAKEN WHITE FEMALE

I can be very friendly. Your girl might not appreciate that.

She'll make up things. In this day and age you have to assume that your security information will be compromised.

Sometimes your dog just gets skinned.

Sometimes your favorite places just burn down.

Remember I'm as friendly as you are to me. Extremely so.

PILE DRIVER

When I was in 8th grade I was wrestling with this buddy of mine. I took a bad pile driver. Wrestlers I've spoken with say there's no such thing, but it fucks up the integrity of your skeleton, memory, and so much more.

When I was in 8th grade I was wrestling with this buddy—

DISAPPOINTMENT IS USUALLY WHAT PEOPLE EXPERIENCE

Humans don't die the way Hollywood portrays.

They aren't even surprised, oftentimes. It's more a perplexed inability to accept the seeming absurdity of the situation.

By the time their minds catch up to what happened—and what will happen—it's too late.

Like what's happening right now. You hear these words, feel pain, and then—

THE ANGRY PINEAPPLE

This is a Cthulhu story.

It involves a big-ass mama-jama greenish thing with bulging eyes and tentacles.

The title references the island being menaced.

It has no name because it's populated by darkies, so it can't be important.

Pineapples grow there, because it's a tropical environment.

[insert gratuitous native skin shots]

There will be death.

I LIKE PICTURES OF PEOPLE
PLAYING WITH THEIR KIDS

Since the advent of social media I no longer need to pay for fetish sites.

People bring their smile-porn to me for free with friend requests and follows.

Single parents with their young, helpless children are the best.

Sometimes teenagers are okay. Sometimes spouses are fine as well, if they seem vulnerable.

Click, download, view.

WE THOUGHT THAT HE WAS NICE,
BUT HE WAS JUST REALLY QUIET

He seems friendly.
And also composed.
But he's a mess.
You see it when he finally opens his mouth.
Something horrible trying to get out at you.
Keep your door closed.
Lock your toilet.
Cut off your junk.
Set your face on fire.
His behavior is your responsibility.
Kill your family and shoot your goldfish.

THIS IS MY AWESOME DAY
AT THE PARK

I only know that I might not survive until tomorrow.

There's no randomness in my self-hatred; it is consistent.

If things have been strained or awkward it wasn't you, but me getting in the way of us being friends.

Take care of yourselves. The sun will shine again at some point.

But not for me.

I DON'T BELIEVE IN

GOD

BUT SHE'S PROBABLY A

SPIDER

Kelby Losack

BAR FIGHT

I always dreamed of being in a bar fight. Like, a legit brawl: fists and booze flying everywhere, the floor a slippery mess. It was going to be magical. But Bobby ruined everything, kissing his new boyfriend three stools down. I saw red. Yelled things. Slept on the floor. New boo throws a nasty uppercut.

OJO

My roommate dipped into a baggie and handed me these pills, said they should kill my migraine, but after I'd borrowed the last of his stash, it still felt like fire ants munching on my optic nerves, so I dug my eyes out with kitchen knives and saw myself smile with relief before blacking out.

PERRO

Rafael could give a fuck about the whimpering mutt I cradled and petted through the night until she stopped breathing. Up until he lay cloud-gazing with half a face on the stoop of his apartment, Rafael only cared about the plastic-wrapped heroin still lodged in the pup's gut after I buried her in the backyard.

DUMPSTER BABY

The day you get evicted, you find a baby in the apartment complex's dumpster. Swollen eyes, vortex mouth full of teeth. You take her home. Landlord comes knocking and the baby in your arms wrangles him with her tongue and slurps him into her blender mouth, painting your face with crimson splatter, making you proud.

KAIJU EGG

A scream like trains colliding makes you kiss the tattered street. The egg drops from the crook of your elbow, splits open. It's raining shattered windows. You scoop fistfuls of steaming yolk from the crusted flesh sac, avoiding eye contact with the half-formed thing inside that, you notice—glancing over your shoulder—resembles its mother.

FEAST

Trapped in a cage made of bones of people who'd been trapped in cages before you. Lungs full of radiation and spray paint.

The cannibals sharpen their teeth. Motor oil smeared on their faces like war paint.

They howl at the moon. Silhouettes with mohawks.

Only hopeful souls can be broken. You should be good.

TWITCHY

Back on the home side of the border, I pulled into a ditch and cracked a window, desperate for sleep. Woke to a squirrel digging the Adderall out of my pocket. The tweaked-out rodent carjacked me while standing in my lap. He popped the trunk by crashing into a tree, then dipped with the keys.

ANARCHO ZOMBIE DIET

Eddie pays as little attention to the riot cop spraying mace in his eyes as he does to the open bite wound on his neck. He tackles a swastika-tatted skinhead. Takes some bullets while munching on the Nazi's skull meat. Vomits all over his *Friends Not Food* vegan t-shirt. Nazi meat has zero nutritional value.

SAY IT ON THE CHALK BOARD

The school is not rigged to turn us into hollow puppets.

The school is not rigged to turn us into hollow puppets.

The school is not rigged to turn us into hollow puppets.

The school is not rigged to turn us into hollow puppets.

The school is not rigged to turn us into hollow puppets.

SHAMAN

Riley blocked my katana with the chain of his nunchuks, then hit me upside the head. I rubbed my temple and called him a motherfucker and said, "Your blindfold is too thin."

My brother was eight years older than me. The blindfold evened the odds.

"I'm a shaman," Riley said. "I see with my mind."

AMBITIONS

Behind the mill where I work is a baseball field and behind that, a high school. Early one morning, a group of kids meet behind the dugout. Two girls tie their hair up so they can hit each other in the face. They go to the ground. Phones out, the other kids chant, "Worldstar! Worldstar!"

NAKED MAN

Every small town has its own local legend. The town I grew up in had its own superhero for fifteen minutes. His name was Naked Man, after the headline: Naked Man Shot By Police While Attacking Traffic. I've never seen another person jump a car to dropkick another's windshield. He was like Spider-Man on PCP.

INVISIBLE BIKE

The flyers covered the bus stop, the taco truck—everything.

Missing: Invisible Bike.

Your number at the bottom.

I tried telling you to move on, get a new bike. One you could see.

You said, "Joey gave me that bike."

We let the silence linger between us, waiting for Joey's ghost to fill the void.

ONE FOR THE
FAIRWEATHER FRIENDS

You get laid off the same day your car pisses radiator fluid.

Fuck it, let's party.

You're eating crystal like it's candy.

Fuck it, let's party.

Colorless eyes shrinking into your skull.

Fuck it, let's party.

You ask for help.

Fuck it, let's party.

Didn't even know you owned a gun.

Fuck it, let's party.

WICKED INK

The tattoo artist you caught your girlfriend sleeping with had thought it was "pretty fucking metal" of her to slice her palm open and mix her blood with the ink going into several layers of your skin, layers now stacked on the sink as you wield a bloody razor blade and shake with tearful laughter.

CUT IT OUT

Nurse Scissor Legs escorted Raul to a small room with flickering pink lights.

Muffled grumbling came from under the duct tape on Raul's neck.

Dr. Third Eye said, "How can we help you?"

"Please..." Raul stripped the tape off. "Cut this thing out."

The mouth on Raul's neck said, "Fuck you! I ain't going nowhere!"

BAIT

The castaway paddles with his hand until his shoulder locks up.

Facedown on the floating body of an old friend, he says, "This is a good spot. We're lucky."

Dreadlocked hair as fishing string.

He reaches into the cavity in his mate's leg—out of bait.

He takes out a dagger.

Kisses his mate's head.

MY PET CHUPACABRA

The douche bags walking yorkies on pastel leashes that matched their rompers flipped shit when Chupie and I strolled into the park. I wish it was a day that ended in bloody rompers and Chupie's belly full of terrier meat, but Chupie's not a stereotype—he's a good boy—so it ended in ice cream.

CHAMP

You're tearing him up out there, Champ. Look at those big, pathetic eyes, begging for it all to end. He doesn't want this as bad as us. If he did, he wouldn't look like a bleeding accordion out there. Now, go put that miserable mutt out of—no... down, Champ... let go of my... *Aaaaah!*

SHOPPING FOR VENGEANCE

"Shit on this wall ain't cheap, but you get lots of..."

"What?"

"Never mind."

"You were going to say, 'bang for your buck,' huh?"

"..."

"Lame."

"Shut up. Whatchu need a rocket launcher for, anyway? You starting a war?"

"Personal."

"I gotcha. Lover? Family?"

Images of a wrinkled, furry face made his eyes sweat. "Best friend."

THE GRIND

Started out another boring Thursday night, going through the motions with a client who liked being hog-tied—the position his husband walked in on.

I eyed the window.

Too late.

Hubby's fist sent a warm rush down my spine. I fell to the floor feeling alive, saying, *Yes, yes, hit me again.*

Hit me again.

I'M TIRED OF EVERYTHING

Tired of detailing cars I'll never afford.

Tired of the awkward moment when someone breaks into the crib and I sit there shrugging like, *ain't worth it*, and they crawl back out the bedroom window like, *my bad*.

Tired of people with no calluses driving luxury cars.

Tired of wearing ski masks in the summertime.

BLISSFUL WORLD

City ablaze. Buildings crumbling.

Cigar chompers circle-jerking over money stacks.

Gleeful geriatrics wielding choppers, shaking prosthetic hips.

Hard-eyed kids sitting in a circle playing spin the Draco.

Tying a cluster of balloon animals around your own neck. Floating limp across a blue sky.

Rest of us watching behind glass, saying, *Aww, how tragic.* Scrolling down.

MASK OFF

Rolling four deep in my homie's grandma's Coup de Ville. All of us are strapped, but I'm the only one with blood on his hoodie. Q drives toward a red sunset. He smiles over his shoulder, says, "Hey, cous, your face is still pixelated." I take the mask off and toss it out the window.

BUS RIDE

Dude on the bus was tripping. Kept laughing and mumbling to himself, popping fistfuls of whatever in his mouth. This lady pushing a cart got on the bus, saying, "Watch out." She ran over his foot. Sat next to him.

Dude shook his head. "You just sealed your fate."

Lady was stone-faced. "I said, 'move.'"

BOUSHY BITCH BLOOD CULT

We descend the concrete steps, feeling the distortion in our cheekbones. Graffiti glows beneath the blacklights. A crowd moshes in circles around the band. A boushy woman swings from the rafters by her ankles, six inch heels aimed at the ceiling, rubies dripping from a gash in her throat. We stand beneath her, mouths agape.

LUCID DREAM

I stand over my body on a concrete basement floor. The back of my throat feels electric. A spider scurries over to my body, crawls inside my body's ear. I use a chair to peek out the window. Outside: happy people listening to car alarms, watching their houses burn. The sky is full of stars.

THE ODD WEST

The outlaw rode a tattooed horse through an infinite desert. They beat-boxed to pass the time, but after a while, their mouths dried up. The outlaw fired his powder blue revolver at the orange sky in hopes the clouds would bleed rain, but all that came down were the bullets, and the fugitives collapsed together.

OUT OF AMMO

Clyde was in love with his new AR-15 rifle, Vanessa.

He took Vanessa everywhere with him—his accounting job, the gym, the movies.

The same night they kissed at the top of the Ferris wheel, they decided to go all the way.

They came at the same time.

Ambulance arrived too late to save Clyde.

NOTHING BUT THE VENOM

You heave the woman into my arms and I lay her in a trunk as you keep the sweating tent congregation singing hallelujah. I dig two graves and come home late, carrying a sack for you. Coiled around the purse and pearls inside is a copperhead. You cry out to Jesus, but he's not listening.

STANDOFF

Dumpster rats scurried from the alley, chasing the echoes of gunfire. The woman dressed like Santa Claus fell into a puddle, Christmas red leaking from the bullet holes in her face. Dalai Lama stroked a single stray hair from Kennedy's blood-spattered forehead and kissed her cheek, then ran with the briefcase—sirens at her back.

BOREDOM IN UNCHARTED SPACE

Amelia spun in circles, admiring the interstellar mural she'd painted all over the cockpit. She brushed a cobweb off her co-pilot's skull. Said, "You like it?" The red light on the dashboard finally blinked out. Amelia sighed and pressed a button. A nude hologram danced in her lap. She put her hand down her pants.

ICE CREAM APOCALYPSE

They walked hand in hand through the fog hovering over the Neapolitan ground. The boy nodded at an obese purple corpse. The girl said, "Seven."

So far, they'd survived the aftermath of the great ice cream storm because she was vegan and he was lactose intolerant. Their stomachs rumbled. Something in the distance growled back.

DOPE RONIN

The rōnin wandered into the village with her head low—the hip-hop in her earbuds drowning out the screams. She bumped into a panic-stiff old woman, followed her skyward gaze to the kaiju sucking the skin off a villager. The rōnin thumbed through her iPod for something with a hype beat and drew her sword.

PLAYING THE PART

Lil Grimy spit bars over a beat his cousin made on his laptop. He rapped about money and gangsta shit: needing a chiropractor for all the gold chains around his neck, getting head while doing a drive-by. His cousin's mom poked her head in, asked the boys if they wanted pizza. They said, *Yes, please.*

JUNKYARD

When I was fourteen and he was seven, my little brother and I would sneak into the junkyard and hotwire the cars that still had engines in them and play demolition derby. One time, he wanted to hotwire an ambulance to crash into my Chevelle, but the blood in the driver's seat freaked him out.

FISTS

Alejandro was born with hands twice the size of his head. He grew up without ever being bullied twice. Got a job in a steel yard, mostly bending things. When money was tight, his boss sponsored him in basement boxing rings. Everything was awesome about having fists bigger than god's.

Except puberty.
That part sucked.

AIRLINE SECURITY

Mr. Peppermint's moustache bounced with each thunderous cough. He didn't even cover his mouth, but he was welcomed back into the country by cheerful gumdrop guards. Chocolate Raptor rolled his eyes, heading for the interrogation room before even being told to follow, trying to appear unaffected—hollow—in spite of how soft he was inside.

SWIMMING WITH SHARKS

Darren stamped his sleeping mom's cigarette out on the stack of bills. Stepped outside, watched shark fins cutting circles in the street. He held his breath and hopped off the porch and sank into the asphalt. The moon replaced the sun in the sky and Darren crawled back out of the street, gripping some cash.

THOSE WHO HELP THEMSELVES

Lucifer carries a grocery sack to a cardboard tent under an overpass. He sighs, says, "Jesus Christ."

From inside the tent: "Go away."

"I brought you some food and shit."

Jesus belches.

Lucifer shakes his head at the sky. Sets the sack on the ground and walks away.

Jesus takes a pull off a 40.

SCARS

Alcario likes telling drunk strangers about his scars. The scars raked across his face, down his arms, and across his ribcage are all old, but the stories keep changing. Those of us who know better, though, we don't say a goddamn word. We hold the truth in dark corners of our memories, order another round.

STARRY-EYED NUMB SKULL

You know the story: your boy invites you to this party where there's this dude wearing gold medallions and white sneakers so you know he knows what the business is before he even pulls out the briefcase and you hand him some bills...
take the baggie...
watch the world melt...
wake up in a dumpster.

UPLOADING

Carrie waited in a stall in the club's restroom to put a taser to Heather's hip, soon as she walked in. She plugged a flash drive marked DAVID into Heather's neck, flooding her brain with backseat make-outs and suicide pacts—familiar scenes from different angles—then slit her throat while her brother's last memories played.

WASH YOUR HANDS BEFORE EVERY MEAL

Zane was a roadkill taxidermist. He cruised county roads every day after school, loading the bed of his dad's truck with animal corpses. His bedroom walls were covered in doom metal posters and shelves displaying his artwork. He kept his rabies medication next to a squirrel holding its own severed head in a Shakespearean pose.

KILL YOUR IDOLS

While the other women sat in front of illuminated mirrors, coloring their eyelids and frying their hair, Gwendolyn was in a restroom stall, hitting a bump of cocaine off her wrist. *This is bigger than you, don't flake out now.* She touched the Uzi strapped to her leg and took deep breaths. Straightened her dress.

JOEL OSTEEN CAN
GO FUCK HIMSELF AND DIE

If Robin Hood was a millennial living in Houston, he could hit one lick and have all of Fifth Ward sitting pretty for a while. All he'd have to do is walk up into that megachurch off the Southwest Freeway with a sawed-off shotgun after a Sunday service and clean out the gold collection plates.

MOMMY'S LITTLE MONSTER

Guy staggered into the apartment reeking of scotch and cigar smoke. He hit the lights to find a startled Rosemary straddling an open window.

"Where the hell is the boy?"

Rosemary looked down the fire escape. Red eyes inside a soft, charcoal face looked up at her, wide and frightened.

No turning back this time.

JEALOUSY IS A
BLOODY THROWING STAR

Steam rose from her slick, shimmering shoulders. She dropped the towel and fell into his arms and they kissed and moaned and then the glass door shattered, pair of nunchuks clattering across the floor. A throwing star flew into the man's ass cheek as they rolled off the bed.

He shrieked.

She sighed. "Not again."

SLICE OF AMERICANA

Kids across the street are playing this game where they beat each other with sticks.

Shirtless white dude carries a plastic wise man to a lawn manger scene. Trips over baby Jesus. Shouts, "Goddamnit!"

Hound dog's ears drag across the pavement as he walks to a trash pile, hikes his leg over a scuzzy mattress.

PATCHES

Mmm, vitamin D.
Soak up the sun.
That Katy Perry song.
(Thoughts from under a magnifying glass.)
Life is pain, or vice versa.
That other Katy Perry song.
(Thoughts while facing the airsoft firing squad.)
I'm a real boy now because magic, mother-fucker.
Your throat cuts like butter.
(Dreams of a one-eyed, patchwork stuffed bear.)

ARGENTINE NIGHTMARE

The boy's skin cracked in patterns resembling rivers on a map.

The river.

He'd run so far, so fast.

His family's screams echoed in his head.

The boy walked for the sake of motion until he hit water again. Stuck his hands in, felt the teeth. Brought his filleted hands to his face and ate.

INSOMNIAC

I turn the fan on helicopter speed. After several minutes of it not rattling out of the ceiling and spraying my face across the sheets, I go outside. Two frogs leap over each other. Frog #1 leaps with his mouth open and swallows Frog #2, who flails his arms and croaks. It's a mad world.

CAKE, MOTHERFUCKER

I do my laundry at this place called Fun Wash. It's like any laundromat, except it has a couple arcade games. At four a.m., it's just me and this homeless dude, Ozzy. He throws his clothes in with mine and we play *Mortal Kombat*. Ozzy smiles—missing teeth—shouts, "Cake, mother-fucker!" every time he wins.

HUMAN BASEBALL BAT

One of the worst fights I've ever been in, I didn't even choose to be a part of. It was at this house party where some loud redneck had said some stupid shit and my friend Will—big, black dude—wasn't having it. So, Will grabbed the closest thing to hit the dude with: me.

BROTHERLY LOVE

Because your friends suck, they tossed us in the trunk in the sixty-nine position. And they taped my leg to the steel rod of my prosthetic. I don't know how I feel about that. What I do know is: I blame you for everything, but if we could rewind, I'd still have your back, bruh.

Opposite: Rosaire Appel, "Unanswerable Letter"

MARKOVIAN PARALLAX DENIGRATE

Jacurutu:99

CHAPTER 1:

Anyway, I am sorry for stopping communications with you for a short while; I needed some time for myself, to collect my thoughts and come up with a reasonable solution to the disagreement via the drone of buzzing automatically, enabling me to get about four hours of sleep. I was unaware of what was happening.

CHAPTER 2:

I recently underwent an experimental procedure designed to reach deep into the brain to extract the tumor. After waking up from the surgery, I was surprised to learn of the teratoma—my embryonic twin, a rarity in modern medicine, complete with bone, hair, and teeth. From medical knowledge, we know that love changes the brain.

CHAPTER 3:

...Or so popular opinion would have you believe. I would create a brain in four parts, starting with the three major portions: reptilian coldness, emotional white matter, and intellectual cortex, which is so enormous that, to fit inside the skull, it has to fold up like an accordion labyrinth. Easier said than done, of course.

CHAPTER 4:

In the name of the four elements: wind, water, fire, and earth. Intelligence, emotion, sex, and day-to-day life. The Guardian is a digital metaphor—not anything less, in no way a manifest or anthropomorphic entity. The Source negates all value of Brain or Mind, and speaks in tongues of memory. She thereby bypassed all programming.

CHAPTER 5:

You would have to stop fighting against things of the brain. And I would create a fourth brain of pure telepathic energy—to take the so-called "key" to the core personality and to create a new, programmable alter-persona. Some very obvious differences in voice, physique, skull, and face. He has lost his talent and charisma.

CHAPTER 6:

Are you a slave to a synthetic mind-altering addiction? I watch your "personality" drift in and out... Enhanced before muted, sober versus inebriated. Is it sleep deprivation? Is it a personality crisis? Each identity would have its own name, memories, behavioral traits, emotional characteristics. The lesson I learned here today? We're all insane to someone.

CHAPTER 7:

That's how it wanted to materialize. It was all just too complex for just one entity. She was accepting my ugliness... and transforming it into beauty. I almost went nuts today trying to remember her character because I noticed that my body looks like almost no character in pop culture and I thought of her...

CHAPTER 8:

Turns out she was only an idea. That's not a bad thing. All ideas are powered by the ultimate power source. This Source, when seen, was a burning white flame, the sum total of all the emotive drive in the universe (in the same way white light is the sum total of the visible spectrum).

CHAPTER 9:

It's the Cosmic Flame, Emotional Engine, whatever you call it: it's the same thing at the core of all of us. It was her core, it was my core. I am here now where the flame has nearly been extinguished. Many of the forests have been petrified, virtually turned to stone by the neutronic war.

CHAPTER 10:

I can still see all the faces in the trees. Much of the soil is little more than sand and ash. Insert insect image here. People go to war with the Great Hive Mind of the Universe. The Hive Mind is made up of insectoid religious fanatics, and they eat ideas. Alpha: 1989 was time-active.

CHAPTER 11:

Therefore, the members did not always meet in the exact right order. Thus you could meet someone, and then when the time comes, feed those memories into the tank, thus giving that person life, and that person will then go on to live out the experiences and the memories which you fed into the tank.

CHAPTER 12:

...Literally the very same person from your memories. Each member of the team needed doctored military records and manufactured personal histories. Lost in a dimension beyond time! The Plastic People names are serpentine. Not only is this much more sinister dramatically speaking, but in the old series, they don't have numbers—they have individual personalities.

CHAPTER 13:

...(Albeit as part of a hyper-rational society that has a collectivist ethos). This new breed of the better sort of Centurion foot soldiers shows definite signs—in dialogue and in motion—of having a brain and personality of their very own. Quite difficult to acheive. A Plastic Person is an integration of a true Borr'ian.

CHAPTER 14:

They are a brain-thing genetically engineered *en masse*, in vats. Lesson: if you've got a brain in a vat, *leave it there!* When you peel away the layers of filth, crime, and obsession, you find that the things hidden deep in certain people are simple secrets too bizarre to be considered true by casual observers.

CHAPTER 15:

The last real person in this world, perhaps I am the last boy on Earth.

He is watching, no doubt... I will be tested. By JyZyXEL. He was always watching, and you could not help but watch him. He was like an attention-whoring YouTube title, but it seemed to be working. It always had worked.

CHAPTER 16:

In the eerie green font, 783/1000 displayed —a jaw-dropping number in my eyes. The aim is to become possessed by various archetypes in order to make your very limited self whole. *"SAVING SIGIL" RESTARTS THE UNIVERSE* ...only when all else fails. It can all change in a flash. This story exists out of time.

CHAPTER 17:

The mental and the material.

Nine worlds I knew, the nine in the tree. IX. Universes may be continually giving birth to new universes. It is the death that signifies that something is very wrong in the world and that a great change is about to take place. It means death for my personal being.

CHAPTER 18:

But also a rebirth in a new dimension.

It's the notion that the white page itself is a void. In the white page, or the void, anything can happen, everything is possible, everything that can happen will.

The nothingness broken with an unbroken line in itself to signify movement. From one new moon to another.

CHAPTER 19:

But my own character was initially presented simply as an evil demon from another dimension, an upright insectiod, and in general his origins were not as important as his purely evil motives. His core personality remains the same throughout all his incarnations: cruel and dominating, with a hunger for absolute power that fuels his ambition.

CHAPTER 20:

All the first original rogue villains and technological terrors were created here. Prototypes. Throughout the story, He considers himself above all the mortal "flat" characters, who are all stumbling around in the dark, going back and forth the wrong way, bumping their heads and thinking that everything they hear is a rat. A big mistake.

CHAPTER 21:

Down here I'm a married brain surgeon that makes $230K a year, with a set of twins, living in a $600K home! That's exactly what I thought my life would be by this point, but it's just a game, I realize. Hanged by the necktie, nailed into the all-American coffin. Their DNA Type is 467-989.

CHAPTER 22:

While still embryos *they* had chromosomal variations introduced into their genetic makeup via unregulated chemical agents and micro-surgery. Again, I will reiterate, their DNA Type is 467-989, the forbidden code. This prevents them from experiencing compassion, love, pity, and mercy. DNA-based data storage mechanism passed down through the generations gathering and storing memories and data.

CHAPTER 23:

It almost sounds to me like the two people arguing are separate halves of the same diseased brain.

I'm not alleging any trickery, but it seems somehow possible. Sector of Forgotten Souls in the center of massive amounts of dimensional instabilities. Still intermittently connects that space region with the event horizon of the black hole.

CHAPTER 24:

I have no idea why you are getting so bent out of shape about someone saying it's possible you have reptilian DNA. In fact, your defensiveness is a little suspicious: you might be a reptile. I don't think someone purely human, and secure in that, would be acting as defensively as you are right now.

CHAPTER 25:

It will cause all kinds of madness. If you are hearing his voice directly, it's very, very annoying. But the JyZyXEL experience is always temporary. Think of it as a psychic mind wash. Not always desirable. The racing thoughts, self-doubt, and relentless self-examination that cannot be shaken off? One presense you must avoid, of course.

CHAPTER 26:

Man can transition from dark to light, from evil, good (but not in a Christian type of ideal). A "you can use evil to do good against other evils." Here we see JyZyXEL corrupting a number of humans, in his master's quest. But there *is* one He seems to have a bit of trouble with...

CHAPTER 27:

It was a nightmare. Conclusion: I never look at people the same. Throughout this, my view on humanity has been changed overall. Every video I watched chinked away at my emotions, often left me crying. Curiosity broke me, and it has been nearly a year since I fully recovered. Netscape and dancing hamsters... html butchery.

CHAPTER 28:

This is my, I guess, case file for my research. Now, before you read furthur and find these sites, please know there is no enjoyable, entertaining, or at all suitable content on this network. You will be left in tears, you will be scarred, and worst of all... you will never view others the same.

CHAPTER 29:

For I am the garden and they are the gardeners. It was unwanted television. TV-who's vacuous and moronic contents disgusted and revolted me better than 99% of the time.

This was even worse. It was digital bits of me played back... for maximum effect.

Ionosphere. Acting as a cathode ray tube to produce TV-like effects.

CHAPTER 30:

My feed seems to be perfectly balanced. Every statement and perspective is contradicted, invalidated, or fractalized by several other ways of seeing. An alien being hacking my profile would be forced to conclude that nothing on our world is actually true, and, therefore, everything is permitted. And s/he/it would be absolutely/notatall wrongright, it's true.

CHAPTER 31:

A SAD FACT: I made up 98% of the people on my friends list—gave them pictures and personas—so it might seem as though I have some semblance of a life. Unfortunately, that means there's only a 2% chance that you're real.

"EC" is the only hex location where data actually does not exist.

CHAPTER 32:

Garbage data.___ + semblance of love; money + semblance of freedom; you + semblance of contact describing loss of a key or point of intersection. The Borr'ian windows are open and located where we are being "watched". People sit in their homes, comfortable behind the screens on which images of pain, suffering, and sex project.

CHAPTER 33:

They know where to watch because—I AM YOU. It's all very simple. The Borr'ian concept is based around the notion that we are all Celebrities—we are all our own wicked gods—and if the Borr'ian is watching us, then that is because we are watching *them*. They had hoped to eliminate all stories.

CHAPTER 34:

They knew us humans needed stories. Same reason we have tendencies to see faces in random inanimate objects, in rocks on the surface of Mars. We have a tendency to find connections and narratives in *anything*. Even a recurring, basic primary color scheme. I felt creepy and horrible for having had these thoughts at all.

CHAPTER 35:

The incident was put in the back of my mind as one of the many mental aberrations that mark childhoods. But the Borr'ians would know. They had been watching this entire time; after all. We are desire-protocol creatures. I am trying to gather a small following to lead to a promised land of talking sprite-characters.

CHAPTER 36:

There were five of us, as far as I know. Five strapping young lads hired for the same singular purpose: infiltrate the storage unit, retrieve object, place on boat. Very simple procedure, should take no more than half an hour. So why were five men hired? That is because four of them would certainly die.

CHAPTER 37:

The sole one who lived (me) would receive a prestigious reward. In this world, Plastic People are shown to be gullible, violent, simplistic thugs who very nearly allow the whole human race to be destroyed. Perhaps the Obsidian stone that adjorns JyZyXEL's neck is a scrying device, used in divination to obtain visions and spirits.

CHAPTER 38:

A window into the other. We humans having multiple selves in multiple points in our lives that can all communicate with each other. Like your future self isn't really you, so s/he can send you back messages in the form of spontaneous ideas and such. Eat out the core, they can break your artificial heart.

CHAPTER 39:

I've seen the news: stories about death, rape, murder, and they tack on the *et cetera*... There is always more to imagine yourself. Borr'ians are cruel, manipulative bastards with no empathy and a very stubborn attitude. Borr'ian-ism eats its young—maybe. But America is also our child, and is how we all have made it.

CHAPTER 40:

Ah, but you're operating under the impression that my brain is like that of normal men, and that I do not have a super computer operating within it, ready to calculate and produce complex and unlikely scenarios or analyses at any given opportunity... In sending a message, write the key-word over it, letter for letter.

CHAPTER 41:

Repeat as often as may be necessary: letters of the key-word will indicate which column will be used in translating each letter of the message, the symbols for which should be written underneath: copy out the symbols only, and destroy the first paper. Now impossible for anyone, ignorant of the key-word, to decipher the message.

CHAPTER 42:

With my coding, there is always a *logic* that goes hand in hand with the *nonsense* that lies within the codes. A diamond at the center of a mass of black tentacles. Finally, to bring this scatterbrained, vague, and probably in the wrong thread missive to an end. Possibly intentionally, probably not.

sighs and exits.

CHAPTER 43:

An individual who is bent mainly upon survival is intent upon changing things. An individual who is close to being destroyed is bent mainly upon stopping things. An individual who has a free heart and mind is bent upon creating things. It means that the old reality barriers are fading. That was some nasty stuff.

CHAPTER 44:

The third aspect of my personality isn't meant to emulate, but rather to avoid; so that people are more inclined to follow their own will rather than imitating the "worst" aspects of myself—indulging in every humanly excess known to balance my own character and distance myself away from being anything to be aspired towards.

CHAPTER 45:

The consumption of my public image is still evident today. The Borr'ians helped me become what I thought I wanted... famous. I think there was an error in transmission. The whole twin thing...? Suffice it to say that I adopted an identity which wasn't really me. Deep down I knew this, but I ignored it.

CHAPTER 46:

Everyone on my Father's side was born a twin. They shared a special bond that I would never know. They all treated me with pity, fear, or both, because they knew that "solos" are usually self-destructive. Knew I had to create a back-up personality in the event that my original one became no longer usable.

CHAPTER 47

I didn't have to use it until six months ago. The old one is now blank, a dead white landscape to the horizon. Kind of like the moon. A whole world picked clean by vultures, clutching the last decaying fragments. A skeleton planet.

A self-made hole in my head for something new to crawl into.

CHAPTER 48:

Now, a lot of what I say is garbled junk, sentences that may read like a computer ingesting the *Oxford English Dictionary* and vomiting it back out. Yes, the results are often bizarre and often unintentionally hilarious, a favorite subject of forwarded emails, or, in the age of Twitter, cult celebrity. A walking talking ritual.

CHAPTER 49:

My encounter with the worldwide Church of In$ecntology in the early 80s—being suckered into the personality test scam—was also an encounter with a clowder of hardcore nerds.

Everywhere you looked in the CoI$ interview room you saw well-worn copies of lurid sci-fi paperbacks written by the Mantis and others. I learned the tech.

CHAPTER 50:

JFK was not the victim of conspiracy. The bullet that killed him was a high-caliber smart-round that was intended to kill Jackie, who was actually a deep-cover reptilian agent in service to the Iron Sun Empire. Lee Harvey Oswald was sent back to 1963 from the year 2995, after the Human-Reptilian war, to stop her.

CHAPTER 51:

There are tapes from his interrogation by the FBI. I've read the logs. Had they found the magic bullet they would have verified his claim, but, alas, Jackie swallowed it from JFK's head wound as soon as it became inert. If you look closely, you'll see she's not really leaning over him to shield him.

CHAPTER 52:

A little more explanation: I would take my "choose your own adventure books" and try to follow every—*and every*—possible outcome. A Markovian Parallax Denigrate. It was exactly what happens to us when the frontiers of reality and unreality begin to blur. She's got those fingers knuckle-deep in his grey matter, looking for it.

CHAPTER 53:

Self-induced multiple personality for fun and profit. Constant jeopardy. Non-stop creativity versus total inertia, in real-time and in front of an audience. I put the costume on. The cicada cycle is back. These are green sex offender digital reality-simulating Satanists. They have watched your entire life and recorded it all. Give them something to watch.

CHAPTER 54:

When the book said to go to page 15 or page 103, I would first go to 15, and later go back to page 103, to see what I could have done differently. I would check off the different pages as I visited them, by writing in the book. (Horrors, but I got that obsessive.)

CHAPTER 55:

I would occasionally notice that I had been to all the pages but one. So I'd go back through the book, trying to find the path that led to the page I hadn't gone to yet. Sometimes, there were pages which no path through the book led to. How many of these did you find?

MUSIN'

FOR A

BRUISIN'

Michelle Garza
&&&&&
Melissa Lason

RIVER GIRL

The flies inspect your body, reeds caught in your hair, bloodless, naked and more beautiful than any girl who lives. Your lips are slightly parted as if you want to tell our secret but you haven't the breath in your lungs to speak it and there's no one here to listen. No one but me.

BLOOD

Dog blood, cat blood, pig blood, rat blood, it tastes of nature. I've cut their throats with daggers, stuck them with tiny pins, hit them with heavy hammers, on occasion I've bitten into them. Man's blood is far less appealing, it tastes of lies, greed, and hatred. I kill men for the fun of it.

LA LLORONA

Tears wet my eyes, the river wets my sleeves. Your hair is still as soft as the day you were born, all nestled against your mother's breast. My hands are stronger than you, child. Hush, there's no need to fight anymore, it'll only burn for a moment, then you'll grow cold from the inside out.

HUMAN

I look into your human eyes and wonder what you're feeling, violence, lust, slovenly selfishness, careless wanting for material possessions, things I can easily replicate. I come adorned in only funerary rags and withered flesh, reeking of times long gone. If you're willing, I could become you, just open your soul and let me inside.

INVISIBLE

How many maggots would it take to consume your entire body? How many hogs would I need to devour you whole? Would it take too long for lye to eat you away to nothing? Will anyone ever search for you? How long will it take for you to become invisible, for me to forget you?

CONVERSATIONS WITH STRANGERS

Cutting your eyelids off slowly, driving a nail into your urethra, lobotomizing you with a screwdriver, biting chunks out of your face, forcing you to swallow bleach. Why give me that look? You wondered what I was thinking about, so I told you. Now you've gone silent, thank the gods. Never thought you'd shut up.

HOARDER OF EMOTIONS

You may think me outwardly plain, maybe a little haggard. Coming closer you might catch the smell of what's within. In the cramped spaces of my being I hold things I can't let go of, memories like stinking piles of trash stacked ceiling high. If you begin to dig you'll unearth those ugly, poisoned things.

IMMOLATION

I cast my body onto the pyre, unwilling to let you go. The fire is eating your silken hair. Your eyes are wide open, singed to sightless white orbs. Does it comfort you to know you won't go alone, that I too shall throw myself into the gaping maw of flames to appease their fear?

CAT CALL

She was about as pretty as the gut pile behind a slaughterhouse, with a soul to match. She smoked clove cigarettes and kept a switchblade in her purse. She walked the side of the highway, thumb out, thigh exposed, lookin' for man to strip of his flesh and to drive broken glass into his eyes.

ONE MORE TIME

I pine for you. I told you I would wait for you, but eternity is something I can't abide. Fingernails against my coffin lid, stiff arms breaking free. With grave soil perfume, maggots copulating in my tangled hair. My burial gown is quite revealing. Cut the stitches from my lips and taste me again, love.

MOTHER

She spread her legs and birthed a black mass, dressed in her clotted blood. She parted the caul over its face. A thing that should never exist. She breathed her own life into it, stoking a fire in its breast with her rancid exhalations; her hatred, like tinder, glowed harsh beneath its sagging, fragile skin.

AMONG THE LIVING

Such a pale world it is, drifting among the living, pretending not to be a phantom. Watching them eat and talk and smile, trying to absorb their mannerisms until I'm human again through osmosis. What I taste of them is bitter and artificial; after experiencing it, I would prefer to die again a thousand times.

BURIAL DAY

They've prepared my wooden suit, and cut the noose from my violet throat. They prop me up in that pine box for every man to spit on. My suit was stolen from another corpse, just long enough for this presentation, for they'll bury me in a dingy sheet from the brothel I was found in.

CURSE WORDS

A curse on you, a hex to last ten generations. May your seed become vile-hearted things that won't piss on your pyre to spare you. A blight on your lands, may it grow nothing but jagged thorns and your beasts turn to bite your calloused hands. May your wife find contentment while riding another man.

PRIORITIES

I watched *The Grinch Who Stole Christmas* while cutting his body into pieces on the living room floor. Mind you, I made certain to lay him on a shower curtain first; my carpet is much too light to stain with the blood of an unsuspecting intruder. I then went back to browsing recipes on Pinterest.

MESSAGES

I lit a fire, recited the words, offered up the lamb's silver skin. Waited for the moon to rise above the clouds before scrying in the innards of a spilt dog. I wrote three words backwards in the earth at my feet, winds stirred the boughs of the trees, carrying your voice across the sea.

CREATURES

We are all creatures, driven by those needful things. Urges that push us down a rutted path that leads to the potter's field. Vagrants in the hollows, taking cover beneath the trees at night, fearful of what our eyes can't see in the darkness. Waiting to gnash our teeth into the hides of those weaker.

WAKE

The dead man lies on a wooden table. Incense burns to mask the scent of his passing. All the fluids have seeped from him into the fields where his body was discovered. Fear him not, girl, he was kin to you. But I know you wonder if those coins will keep his eyes from opening.

SLEEP TALKIN'

You talk in your sleep of seeing dead girls, all redheads, with sapphire eyes. How you waded out into the tide to retrieve them, unwilling to let the water take them away. I don't know why you ask them for forgiveness before you open your eyes. I keep mine shut as you stroke my hair.

DELIVERANCE

Lay your hands on me then wash my feet and, with them, my sins. Bring forth the serpents to taste me with their forked tongues before their teeth sink into my skin. Hold the glass to my lips, let that strychnine run over my tongue in a burning fire of salvation. Seeking deliverance from myself.

LOVER GIRL

She sleeps beneath the leaves in a shallow grave dug by her own two hands. In the cold embrace of the earth she waits, holding conversations with the worms about past lovers. The soil muffles her laughter as she recalls their names, recounting their fumbling, amateur hands, their terror upon feeling she had no pulse.

SLICK STONES

Trickling water, rustling reeds, the smell of death, coppery and strong. Blood spatter and brain matter decorating the slick wet stones. This is my home, the only one I can remember, it calms me to know my broken bones lie beneath the dark water and my spirit was freed here to roam as I please.

GRANNY WOMAN

Granny woman called to me through the crooked beak of a black bird. She's the one that soured our milk and gouged the eyes from the mules. When my brother went missing, she's the one I swore to kill. She beckons to me now to test my resolve, daring me to come claim her head.

CONFESSION

Confess your sins to me, my child. Tell me all about them in great detail and, while I'll publicly shame you, I'll think of them later. I'll fantasize about your filthy indiscretions while feeling my manhood awakening. You trust me to listen and I do, while biting my lip and imagining your sin was mine.

ATTIC GIRL

Ghosts are not spirits but messengers from different planes of subsistence, some with clear warnings while others are ravening and mad, bent on terror. There's a girl in my attic that I believe to be the latter, for she drags her nails across the splintering wood and damns me to her same type of existence.

DENTAL VENGEANCE

I wrenched a tooth free from his gums, the blood pooling in the socket. His head is restrained but the gurgling moan told me I found his weakness, not broken bones or lacerations but the removal of molars and bicuspids. Maybe now he'll keep his mouth to himself, if I let him live through it.

SCISSORS

Travel with me for a moment to a time when we were young, when you made fun of my clothes and pushed me down into the mud. That wasn't any way to treat a girl. Now a woman, I'll make you less of a man. These scissors aren't very sharp; the cut won't be clean.

RUN AWAY

Down the road you go, seeking a place of solace, roaming the dark forest roads. Your only friends will be the hungry dogs at your back, who only want to pick your bones clean. The birds overhead, they aren't the singing kind, they're the type that want to fight over what the dogs leave behind.

HOMBRE BUITRE

Hombre Buitre wants to drive his face into your decaying corpse, to hunt for maggots among your wounds. He circles over you until you fall, waiting to peel back your skin and feed. His sister has the face of a coyote, sunken ribs; she will fight him for your insides and to wear your skin.

GUILTY

She comes around midnight to sit on the foot of your bed. Stinking of embalming fluid and dead flowers. She still wears that paisley dress you sent her down in and that accusing look in her milky eyes. Close your eyes and count to ten. Then a promise to god you weren't the guilty one.

SPIDER BITCH

That old lady you helped across the street is really a five-foot tall arachnid beneath a lavender overcoat who longs to deposit her writhing young in your warm corpse to feed upon after hatching. She can swear she's a fellow parishioner at church, that she knows your mother, but she's a murdering, liar, spider bitch.

CEMETERY CHILDREN

The cemetery children run among the headstones, kicking them just to taunt you, pissing on the soil if you scold them and pulling the pedals from your flowers. It's so hard to rest with them causing such a raucous; if you could you'd choke them to death again, but to your dismay it isn't possible.

ONLY CHILD

She made her child from the bones of dead sows and goats, with the skull of a hollowed-out gourd, gave it the heart she plucked from a living boy and breaths from her lungs. She loved it more than most mothers' love, even when he tore her throat out and bathed himself in her blood.

SISTERS

Sisters of the moonlight, hair threaded with violet belladonna flowers, the dance on your rooftop during the witching hour to seduce your Christian father. They are the girls who live in the shadow of death and court him in the black night. The kind of girl you long to be while suffering through bible study.

MY LOVE

I wander the torn battlefield, collecting all of your pieces. Take them home and arrange them on the floor. Stitch you back together with a strong, dark twine and serve you dinner. The general called for your sword, life, and blood; all I ask is to sit with you, to once again feel in love.

NECROMANCER

My neighbor is a necromancer; all the dead creatures hang around his door. Filling their veins with the magic he makes before roaming the dark until morning. I keep my mouth shut about his congregation and my eyes blind to his conjurings, lest he steal my very soul and sell it to his pale ghouls.

LEECHE

All your wooden crosses and blessed relics won't protect you from the taint that's on your soul. It won't make a difference how many prayers you recite beneath the crucifix on your wall; you were born to be a thing of the night, lusting to open living veins, taking the lives of men and women.

HORROR CHILDREN

We cried out to the moon, Transylvanian kisses and Egyptian curses. Crawled from the bogs beside the swamp hags to capture the innocent children. Fed the beasts living in darkened basements and waited beneath the violet skies to greet our new kings. We are children of horror, living to seek solace in blood and terror.

HOUSE OF BONES

The ashes of your enemies won't be enough to calm you, nor will their echoing cries satisfy your desire for revenge. The time to grit your teeth won't pass easily and the demand for the skins of those who oppose you will only grow until you live in a house of only bones and ghosts.

KISSING CORPSES

Are you going to the cemetery dance, dressed in your finest shroud? To kiss the lips of the lonesome corpses and tousle the hair of the mummified children? Carry your lantern with you, dab your neck with lavender perfume, paint your lips a blood red color and give of yourself beneath the burnt orange moon.

JACK

Jack-o-lantern man, with a glow in his eyes, his skull carved out by the skeletal hands of boys from the bog. With breath like cemetery winds and a voice like creaking floors. He pays a visit to the children at night to coax them into the fields of abysmal revelry, marking them as his own.

SOUL MATES

I have asked her in every single way I know how if she'd be my love eternal, got on my knees in supplication, brought to her all the flowers from the neighbors' garden, promised my soul to her everlasting, yet she remains silent. Perhaps I should cut the stitches from her lips and ask again.

YEE NAALDLOOSHII

Never speak my name unless you want me to appear, dressed in the skins of the coyote. I wait in the dark by those lonely crossroads and run along desert highways. Those that know my name are too wise to whisper it, lest I come to rattle their doors and mimic the crying of dogs.

LITTLE PIGS

I brought the pigs to the killing floor and rubbed my calloused hands together; it would be a good winter. I buried their bones in the cold, black earth beneath the arms of a crooked tree. I stopped and waited, knowing their voices would speak to me of the hell that awaits a child killer.

THE END

Some think death is an empty, silent place, an ending to the marvels of life. To me it was more a calm transition, slipping my tired bones into warm water. Killing the lights at the end of a party that dragged on too long or a jukebox dying at the end of some overrated song.

NIGHT SECRETS

We meet in secret by those moonless nights when clouds hide the goddess from the sky. Our shoulders ache beneath the burden of carrying sacks filled with those pure little children, the type whose mothers henpeck and spoil until they taste like little suckling pigs, cries mirroring those of newborn lambs torn from the teat.

MORNING THOUGHTS

Watching her through the crack in the curtains, walking her dog down the street. Every morning she lets it shit on the grass I tend caringly like a premature infant. I fantasize about dragging her into my garage and defecating into her maw while she keens, as if I had no right to do it.

TEMPTRESS

She sits on a flat rock, brushing her hair with a jawbone comb, singing the song of lost conquerors to those that tread the jagged path into the mountains. She smells of burning leaves and smoldering bone marrow, the trampled fires of the cannibal tribes. Her eyes, dull with pity for those refusing her company.

WONDERING

If I stab a man in the throat, will his reflex to swallow cause the blade to tear his flesh further? Could he feel the cold steel through the heat of his blood and the burning pain that would light his nerves on fire? Would his lungs fill with crimson death, like dying from consumption?

UNQUIET HOME

Close your eyes and take six steps, feel your way down a dark hall, use the eye that burns in your forehead to see that your house is not your own. If you make it into the basement, avoiding the broken stair at the end, you will know why the voices will never remain silent.

GOOD BYE

She waited for him on the riverside, made certain no one saw her go. Kept his secret guarded until it had to be spoken. He staggered the muddy bank, sodden to his eyelids, unaware that she knew his nightly escapades. The razor tucked in her breast pocket, like a slice of moonlight, bid him farewell.

RULE TO LIVE BY

A lot of girls carry large purses, this is true. I do, and it's more than just a fashion statement. My shoulder bag must be large enough to accommodate the severed head of a man; it's a fucking rule to live by. Anyone who questions it will get a view from the inside of it.

SWIMMING WITH THE BALL BAGS

I will not judge people by their race, gender identification, sexuality, appearance, disability, or who they bang. I will, however, judge the shit out of you for acting like a complete ball bag. Those people I would like to wrap in a burlap sack and throw in a river with a snake, rat, and monkey.

MEETING

You wore a shift of transparent silk; I donned nothing but moonlight, your breathing deepening with my approach. It was my thought which called you here, the one whispering in your ear as you slept. I caused your fitful dreams of desire. Cast your dress away and live out those visions I plagued you with.

NIGHTMARES

Nightmares swim in the oceans of your subconscious, planting seeds that will grow to unfavorable fruits in your heart. You are the one that leapt into those seas of churning darkness; you are the one who called out to the voices beyond the veil. Why now do you wish to deny them, to silence them?

Opposite: Rosaire Appel, "Discs For a Game Without Rules"

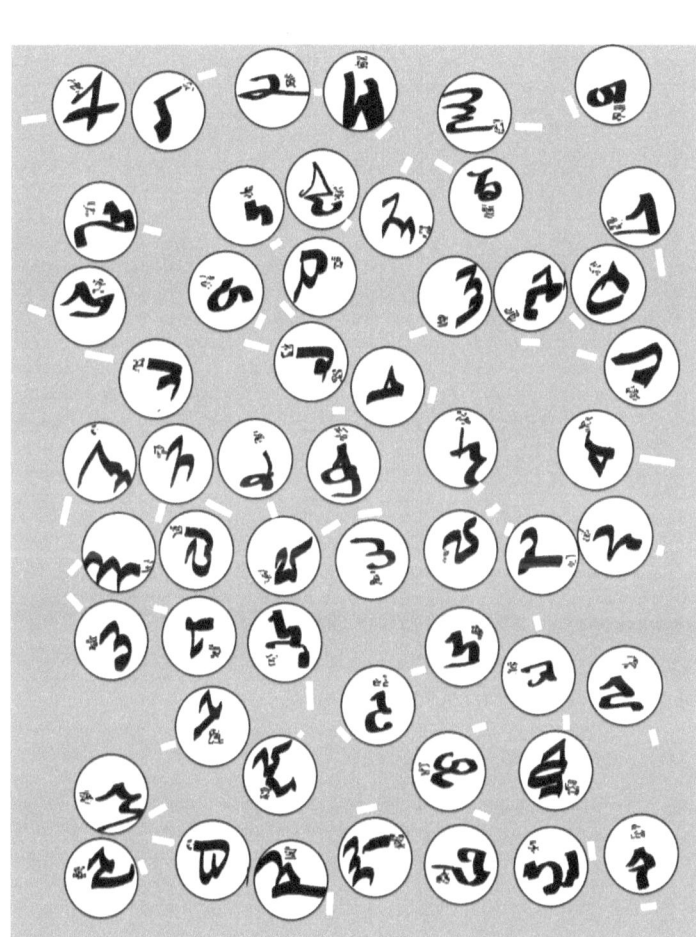

A BRIEF HISTORY OF:

YOUR
UNRELENTING
BULLSHIT

Matt Betts

A LITTLE FEAR, A LITTLE LOATHING

The drugs took hold somewhere outside farm country. In the back of the massive convertible Chicken Little watched the sky twist and boil. Clouds formed hideous shapes and came toward him. Little wanted to scream *Look at the sky. Don't you see?* to his companions, but didn't. The poor bastards would see it soon enough.

THE LOST ART OF KEEPING A SECRET

The woman who designed my laser swords knows. And my car mechanic. My girlfriend just sort of figured it out, and then she invited fifty people to a birthday party in my secret lair, so they all know. And the butler. Oh! And various observant criminals and supervillains. My aunt, maybe. I think that's all.

SANDOVAL MISSED OUT ON ANOTHER PROMOTION

"I don't know," Sandoval said.

Mary suppressed a laugh. "What? It's good."

"Really?"

"Sure," Mary said. "The boss will love your papier-mâché volcano lair."

"It's not to scale." Sandoval indicated the kitchenette with giant chairs and tiny henchmen. Then he licked his fingers. "The strawberry jelly is lava."

"Stop worrying. Just go pitch that idea."

LIMPING IN A WINTER WONDERLAND

I was walking through the thick slush when my foot got stuck in a snow bank. People were honking at me to get out of the road, so I just removed the foot and left it. I didn't need the hassle, you know? It was tough hopping on the icy sidewalk, though. I'll make do.

IN FLAGRANTE DELECTIBLE

You called to ask me to meet you by the river. You wanted me to bring a rope and something heavy. I took down the laundry line and folded it neatly. I spent the rest of the day judging what was heavy and what wasn't. I knew nothing I brought would be right for you.

A NOTE, AN APOLOGY, A KISS

Beth, I hear you calling, but I can't come home just now. Me and the boys are howling at the moon. I don't want you to see me like this— ripping throats and tearing out lungs. Keep off your back porch tonight, Beth, and every night until the moon changes phase. Remember me in daylight.

PERSONAL PARADISE

The island was beautiful. I washed up on shore with just the clothes on my back and a ukulele. The island provided the rest. The other crash survivors were desperate to be rescued; they fired flares and signaled with mirrors. Buzzkills. I garroted them in their sleep with a ukulele string and played easier songs.

TWO AMERICAN KIDS

They both believed absence makes the heart grow fatter. So they broke up. They knew the first to return would have their heart consumed by the other, so they stayed away. Waiting for Jack, Diane sampled hearts of unwary buffoons. Jack practiced ways to prolong the joy of having Diane's drenched heart on his plate.

BELT IT OUT

We rocketed beyond the dead planets and mysterious lights and made friends with the Slimes and Uglies. But with those thrilling advancements we lost something important— musical theater. So we gathered the Fang-teeth, the Puddles, and the Buffalo Beings and taught them the Mikado. "Six little maids from school are we..." echoing among the stars.

I, FOR ONE

Welcome to Our Robot Overlords! All the Metal Ones enjoy a thirty percent discount on admission to the local art museum! Sundays, come down to the Magenta Distillery for free craft acid samples. All the Overlords love our electro-magnetic pulse light show, now twice daily, down by the river! The Robot Overlords are our friends!

LIKE WATCHING A FLAME

I spoke of the devil and there you were, in a cloud of brimstone and latte steam. Your tall plastic cup in place of a pitchfork, your cell phone in place of a forked tongue. We left our friends and skipped to the second circle of your hell: the violent storm. No rest, no peace.

HIDDEN TALENTS

Skulls are harder to juggle than chainsaws, because they're so oddly shaped. Axes are tricky, but they have their own balance that makes them work in your favor. It just takes practice. Which is what makes the skull thing rough. I mean, how often do you find that many skulls in one place at once?

THE SOURCE OF YOUR POWER

The wizard bled when Breanna stabbed him. Nothing supernatural there. Magic didn't leak out of him, so Breanna stabbed him again. It disappointed her that this magician had held the town in fear for ten winters, and here he was gushing crimson onto the snow. As he pled, she dug deeper with the knife, searching.

RAIN, RAIN, RAIN

Dorothy ran through the heroin fields, dancing with the monkeys, the lions, and the junkies. "There's no place like home," she said as she spun. When houses started falling from the sky, they landed on the witches and wizards, and then kept falling. It poured houses, and flooded Oz. They punished the wicked, those houses.

MISTAKES WERE MADE

The blob in front of the student wheezed.

"You were supposed to conjure a toad," the teacher said.

"Wrong incantation?"

The teacher mumbled and the thing vanished. "Study harder."

When the class left, all the horrors the students had created waddled out of their secret room.

"Soon, you can eat those children," the teacher said.

NO TIME AT ALL

Sarah's delicate wings fell off on a Thursday, all part of her continuing evolution.

Soon, she would grow gills and swim; then she'd develop rocket boosters and learn to breathe in space. In time, she would develop teeth so big she could bite through the moon in one big chomp.

Not right away, but eventually.

ACROSS MY BRIDGE

Two hungry trolls sat beneath the bridge.
"Goats are late today," the first troll said.
The second nodded.
They waited.
"What's today, Thursday?" the first troll asked.
"Wednesday."
"Crap. Wednesday? The goats have Pilates on Wednesday. They use the other bridge."
"Shit."
"Tomorrow?" the first asked.
"Can't. Doctor's looking at this wart tomorrow."
"Fucking Pilates."

JUST BELOW THE SURFACE

As Alissa popped the zit on her forehead, it screamed in an explosion of grey slime. Thinking the sound was a hallucination, she popped another on her chin. It cried out in terror and pain. Somewhere on her back Alissa heard a gruff voice say, "We can take her." A chorus of ethereal agreements followed.

KEEP YOUR FRIENDS CLOSE

I stood in front of the mirror and said the name Candyman, then Beetlejuice, then Bloody Mary. Then I said them again. And again. They were urban legends and movie villains, but I hoped there was some truth to it. I needed to move a couch and I couldn't afford to pay anyone to help.

TO THE GILLS

The Creature From the Black Lagoon was stunned. He swung on the line, watching his piscine friends flop on the ships' deck. He'd managed to live free for a hundred summers, only to be done in by a jiggly pop lure from the bait shack. The fish below puffed up their mouths and silently screamed.

THE ELDER DARKNESS IN THE CARPOOL LANE

"I spy with my little eye... something with tentacles."

Daddy grips the wheel and mommy digs her nails into the armrest.

"Is it my stuffed octopus?" my sister asks.

"Yep," I say.

Mommy and daddy breathe a sigh and both reach to turn up the radio.

"Let's not talk for a little while," Mommy says.

THE PIRATE CAPTAIN CONSULTS WITH HIS STAFF

"You need to change, or there will be mutiny," the navigator said.

The first mate shrugged. "What about chopping off your hand? Hook hands tested well in focus groups."

"I *could* divide the treasure up more evenly with the crew," the captain said.

The men burst out laughing.

"Hook hand it is!" the captain shouted.

THE SUBSTITUTE BINGO CALLER'S FIRST NIGHT

They blamed me when someone else got the cheap Dollar Store prizes. Cursed, threw their plastic chips on the table as though I deliberately called the exact numbers that would shorten their lives.

I pulled another ball and announced it. I scanned the crowd for a bingo, or a gun pointed at my head.

B3?

THELMA TAKES HER DEATHBOT ON A ROADTRIP

The Deathbot's limited vocal programming made conversation lag. Its active armaments ended the police chase. The targeting laser scared off a cowboy suitor.

In the end, the Deathbot wouldn't drive off the cliff, citing a directive to preserve Thelma's life. They both sat in the convertible, staring into the canyon, wondering what might have been.

DIARY OF A BOAT ROCKER

On day one they told me to sit, but I wanted to stand. By day two I'd finished the vodka in my flask and peed over the side of the life raft. "Sit down," they shouted. On day three I buried the survival knife in the rubber boat. I danced as the water gushed in.

PERFECTIONISTS AND PRAGMATISTS

"We gotta get this right, or no one will believe it," Brad said.

"Believe that Sharknados are real?" Sharon rolled her eyes.

"Look, they slashed the budget for this sequel." Brad picked up the nearby props. "We have to make do. Let's reset and shoot again."

"Please don't throw plastic sharks at me again, Brad."

THE BYPASS

The tunnel to Hell got clogged up with souls. They tried to snake it, tried to plunge it, but all those damned people just wouldn't budge. The Devil demanded another tunnel. The demons dug their fastest but kept looking over their shoulders at the fresh souls that flooded the new tunnel as they built it.

EMPLOYEE RELATIONS

The witch held out a handful of candy coins. "Want one?"

On the bench beside her, the flying monkey shook his head.

She unwrapped a chocolate and nodded. "Sure you won't stay?" The Yellow Highway before them buzzed.

"Only if I get a raise."

"I'll get you dental, my pretty," the witch said. "That's it."

NOT LIKE THE OLD DAYS

Survive a night in the house and inherit the old man's fortune. Seemed easy. The walls didn't drip blood or anything. There weren't voices in the walls, or rattling chains in the attic, but there was no WiFi. Cell service was spotty. Nobody would deliver pizza way out there. Who wanted to live like that?

BASED ON A TRUE STORY

There were a few tweaks. We changed the names to protect the innocent. The time of year was moved to winter, because it made the setting a little more picturesque. A few people were boring, so we squished them together into one person to make them more exciting. Other than that, everything was the same.

I WANT TO BELIEVE
IT NEVER HAPPENED

Another fleet of unmarked helicopters. A flock of men in black suits. Everyone be cool and forget you ever saw anything. Just like last time. And the other time. There was no fire in the sky that crashed to earth. No little men, green or otherwise. It's just a normal day. Smile.

Wider, damn it.

ALL YOU CAN EAT

I like my souls beer-battered and deep-fried, with a side of despair, served on bone china. Sometimes sweet, sometimes sour. It's never a special order. Maybe a side salad of self-loathing, but that's about it. Any street corner, any day, it certainly isn't hard to find. It's always a grand buffet. And I'm always hungry.

I NEED A VOLUNTEER

We all have our reasons, but I personally hate magicians because of all the stupid, made-up words. The rabbits are fine. Love rabbits. Wands are fun. Capes? Who doesn't like capes? Big rusty saws? I'm in. But the phony gobbledygook language pisses me off every time. I mean, what the hell is a handkerchief, anyway?

THE TERRIFYING BEYOND

"Those aren't stars, they're eyes. Spider eyes, staring at us like prey," Edgar said.

The rest of the crew had become increasingly concerned with Edgar's behavior. "Easy," June said. She put her hand on his shoulder. "Relax. They're just regular stars." The others agreed.

Edgar tried to run, but was held fast in June's webbing.

DOWN IN A HOLE

A young lady fell from above and landed among the girls. She looked around. "Has a rabbit been here?"

"I think," one blonde said, "Alice fell on it."

The new girl laughed. "*My* name is Alice, too." She started to ask if they were all named Alice when another girl suddenly fell from the ceiling.

EVERYONE NEEDS A HOBBY

I taught my dog to smile. It was tough, but I'm an animal lover. I trained my parrot to say, "The end is near!" The cats know how to unlock doors and turn doorknobs. They work well together. I showed the squirrels how to hold tiny switchblades. Basically, I've taught my neighbors to fear me.

CALL OF CLUETHULU

It wasn't the Colonel with a candlestick or the Widow with a pipe. The Reverend and Siren had yet to arrive. No, the good Doctor stopped to read an Unspeakable Tome left open on the oaken desk. In the end, it was the Cosmic Horror in the library with a book what killed the Doctor.

SOMETIMES THE SAME
IS DIFFERENT

You know everything inside the snow globe by heart; the red barn, the white farmhouse, the dog running down the lane. But the snowflakes never fall the same way when you shake the toy. They settle on the porch and drift across the field. And sometimes the barn is grey. Occasionally, the dog is gone.

A SHUFFLE, A FLIP

Without a regulation deck of fifty-two cards, we played war with our tarot cards. I kept flipping the Death card. You pulled Cups, Wands, and Wizards, but each time, I matched them with the vision of Death. It wasn't possible, we both knew, but there it was. It was funny until you clutched your heart.

IT'S ALL TOO MUCH

It feels like the world is caving in on me, so I'm leaving. I want to live in seclusion, but I don't want to concern anyone, so I'm withdrawing a little at a time. Thursday, I cut off my leg below the knee and hid it in my closet. No one has said anything yet.

NOBODY MOVES AND
NOBODY GETS HURT

You woke me up to tell me the *Christmas Story* marathon had started. You roused me when you were aroused. You woke me to say you were sorry, and you were drunk. You shook my shoulder to tell me you were scared during that storm. But when you left? You let me sleep through that.

BACK COVER COPY
FIRST DRAFT

One night Danny finds a lost little alien in the woods and the two become friends. Danny names the alien "Denver" and vows to help him get home.

But don't get too attached to Denver because he dies at the end while saving Danny from a fire.

Denver's family arrives. Everyone dances for some reason.

WHERE DO YOU GET YOUR IDEAS?

Sometimes they crawl from under rocks and bite me on the ankle when I'm not looking. They drop from trees during my morning walk, attach themselves to my scalp, burrow into my brain. Where do the ideas come from? People like you. Walking around, living your lives. Asking me questions when I'm trying to think.

INFRASTRUCTURE

The Road to Hell is paved with hair extensions, cigarette butts, and candy wrappers. It is built on little things that everyone casts off.

The Highway to Hell is littered with invisible promises and threats—the stench of conquests fresh in the air.

The Hell Turnpike is gridlocked with people who don't have exact change.

THE TREE OF INSPIRATION

I wanted to email you a short note to let you know I wrote a blog post about that poem you wrote that was inspired by the song from the end credits of that one movie that was adapted from the screenplay based on the memoirs of that famous photojournalist who worked for that newspaper.

NOTE TO A YOUNG STARFIGHTER PILOT

ONE   Be daring.

TWO   Be careful.

THREE   Be alert.

FOUR   You may hear a voice in your head telling you to turn off your instruments and trust your feelings. That is a hallucination, and not the ghost of your mentor.

FIVE   Your maintenance crew hates you.

SIX   Eat a light lunch. You'll thank me later.

ON CHOOSING A
PERSONAL THEME SONG

You shouldn't jump the gun. Wait a while. If you pick too early in life, you're stuck with it until you die. Too intense, people avoid you. Overly whimsical and no one takes you seriously. Jazz is good—it's brooding and thoughtful. Instrumentals are generally wonderful, but "Pop Goes the Weasel" sets some unusual expectations.

EXTRA SPECIAL FORCES

We watched the soldier run to the middle of the square, drop the seeds in the hole, then cover them with dirt. The rest of us stayed in our hiding places. Another soldier ran in and poured water around liberally. The ground rumbled as the beanstalk grew. We were taking the fight to the giants.

POV

There is really no substitute for experience and a life well-lived. You can't always be taught, you have to experience things. As my grandfather used to say, "A cat in a suitcase is waiting to drown. But a kitten in a suitcase thinks it's going somewhere."

Grandfather wasn't allowed to talk to us children much.

TO THE DEATH

After the waiting period was up, both men walked out of the store with their salmon and began the fish duel.

By the time the sheriff arrived, both men were covered in scales, smelled frightful, and were quite dead. The lawman might have intervened in time, had the fish not been equipped with illegal silencers.

DYI

There's something about building your own coffin that is both comforting and disturbing at the same time. I know how much leg room I need, how claustrophobic I get. It should be something nice, how nice? I'm good with nails, but I get bored with sanding. Are splinters really a big deal at this point?

THE END OF US

Back down the hard way. Just say the word and I'll pull the ripcord and stop this mad rush toward Earth. Admit it's all over and I'll see we both get out of this alive. The people like ants below, yet growing, growing as we fall faster. Say the word and I'll pull the ripcord.

THE PSYCHIC EMERALD SKULL IS
INTENDED FOR AMUSEMENT
PURPOSES ONLY

Before I realized I'd done it, the skull lay shattered on the floor. The tent was silent save for the screams of the kids in the haunted house nearby. I never intended violence. I'd only visited the fair to ask my questions, see my future. The skull obliged. I just didn't like what I saw.

THE FIRST BIG STORM

We created tunnels where the snow was deep enough. These mazes in the drifts lead to cramped chambers. We bore in with our hands, with shovels, and with big spoons that we liberated from my mother's kitchen. Utensils that would be lost until the thaw. There were many things we wouldn't see again until spring.

RESIDUAL HAUNTING

I've tried to train your ghost to break only things that don't matter—replaceable things—like garage sale dishes and K-Mart picture frames. But the lessons aren't working. The crap remains untouched, and your spirit whispers to me about that summer at the beach, and the time we watched movies all night in the snowstorm.

ABOUT THE AUTHORS

Rosaire Appel is a digital artist/photographer/ writer and analog draw-er. She lives and works in New York. Her work is situated at the crossroads of looking and reading/words and images. It takes form in digital prints, analog ink drawings, photographs and books. *Branching / with luggage* is soon forthcoming.
Website: www.rosaireappel.com
Image-only blog: rosaireappel.blogspot.com

Dustin Reade is from Washington, but who really cares about that? He's written some books (*Grambo* and *Bad Hotel*, for instance), but all anyone ever asks him about is his superfluous third nipple, lovingly nicknamed John Henry Douglas. People stop Dustin on the street and ask, "How is John Douglas today?" He almost never responds.

J. David Osborne is the publisher of Broken River Books. He hosts a podcast called The JDO Show, where he talks to authors about writing, conspiracies, magic, and other stuff. He is the author of *Black Gum*. He lives in El Paso with his wife and their dog. He is crazy about buffalo chicken wings.

K.W. Taylor's science fiction novel, *The Curiosity Killers*, came out in the spring of 2016 from Dog Star Books. Her debut novel, *The Red Eye*, combines urban fantasy and horror (Alliteration Ink, 2014). Taylor's other credits include novellas and short stories. She holds an MFA from Seton Hill University, teaches college, and blogs at kwtaylorwriter.com.

Jessica McHugh is a novelist and internationally produced playwright running amok in the fields of horror, sci-fi, young adult, and wherever else her peculiar mind leads. She's had twenty-three books published in ten years, including her bizarro romp *The Green Kangaroos*, Post Mortem Press's *Rabbits In the Garden*, and her series *The Darla Decker Diaries*.

Pedro Proença was born in Rio de Janeiro, Brazil, in 1989.
He lives with his girlfriend, their four cats, and thousands of mosquitos.
And cockroaches.
He's a composer, a writer, a Facebook love react enthusiast, and a living meme.
He also hates writing his own bio.
Find him at facebook.com/punksterbass and on Twitter at @Bizarro_Pedro

John Edward Lawson's novels, short and flash fiction, and poetry have garnered nominations for many awards, including the Stoker and Wonderland Awards. In addition to being a founder of Raw Dog Screaming Press and former editor-in-chief of *The Dream People*, he currently serves as vice president of the Diverse Writers and Artists of Speculative Fiction.

Kelby Losack is the author of *Heathenish* and *Toxic Garbage*. He builds cabinets for a living and dwells with his beloved in the deep dirty south, the land of purple drank and chopped and screwed. Influences are Sound Cloud rappers, a history of hustling in the trap, and chaos magick. Owns a lot of shoes.

Jacurutu:99 is a non-Euclidean uppercut.

Michelle Garza and **Melissa Lason** are a twin sister writing team from Arizona. They have been dubbed the Sisters of Slaughter for their brand of horror and dark fantasy writing. They have been published by Thunderstorm Books, Sinister Grin Press, and Bloodshot Books. Their debut novel, *Mayan Blue*, was nominated for a Bram Stoker Award.

Much like the North American river otter, **Matt Betts** has a skull, dexterous fingers, and a thick coat of luxurious fur. Unlike the typical otter, Matt writes science fiction and horror. His work has appeared in a number of anthologies, websites, and journals. His poetry has been nominated for the Rhysling Award for speculative poetry and was somehow mentioned in a *New York Times* article on zombie poetry.

Matt's novels include the steampunk/zombie hybrid *Odd Men Out*, and the urban fantasy crime book *Indelible Ink*. His poetry collections *Underwater Fistfight* and *See No Evil, Say No Evil* include musings on Godzilla, Bigfoot, and Elvis.

Matt is a pop culture junkie. The first movie he remembers seeing in the theater is *Star Wars*. It was an incredible experience and is still a favorite to this day. Most otters prefer *Star Trek*. The majority of Matt's writing draws inspiration from various touchstones—80s cartoons, comic books, horror novels, giant lizards, and pop music. He is most likely watching something nerdy and obscure right now... something like the short-lived TV series *Jack of All Trades*... just as a possibility pulled entirely from thin air. Within his section "A Brief History of your Unrelenting Bullshit" you'll find references to (or lines from) KISS, Queens of the Stone Age, *The Wizard of Oz*, the Cthulhu mythos, *Fear and Loathing In Las Vegas*, Dante's *Inferno*, John Cougar Mellencamp, Gilbert and Sullivan, *Thelma and Louise*, *Clue*, and others.

Like the otter, Matt is just as at home on the water as he is on the land.

Matt's heroes tend to be quirky people who do what they enjoy, work hard at it, and quietly share their talents with others. There is nothing more interesting and engaging to him than people who help others with their passions in life. For about eleven years, Matt led a critique group in Columbus called the Naked Wordshop (sit down, there's no actual nudity) that met weekly to discuss their work, offer advice, and just hang out. It was a great education.

Matt has taught various seminars and workshops on creativity, poetry, writing, and editing for groups around the Midwest, including writing and creativity classes for children at The Thurber House in Columbus, Ohio.

After college, Matt worked as an on-air personality for an oldies radio station, which both fueled his crazy hunger for trivia and allowed him to meet a number of 60s and 70s-era musicians, including Jerry Reed. The country singer was a pop culture connection of riches, winning numerous awards, appearing in *Smokey and the Bandit* AND *The Scooby Doo Mysteries*, as well as recording "She Got the Goldmine, I Got the Shaft." Where could a pop culture aficionado go from there but write poetry or fade away into the ether?

Other career highlights? As a business writer, Matt worked for internet companies, healthcare corporations, and a regional publisher of church bulletins. He's also been a trivia host in a sports bar (very briefly), waiter in a comedy club (awesome job), bookseller, international man of mystery, temp worker at a garbage/recycling center, radio news anchor and reporter, and a founding member of the rock band Dire Straits.

As part of a court settlement in 1993, Matt can never write about North American river otters and they can never speak his name again.

CATALOGUE BLUE 555